WHITE COLLAR CRIME
LARGE PRINT EDITION

MYSTERY, CRIME, AND MAYHEM
ISSUE 22

LEAH R CUTTER   CHRIS CHAN   CATE MARTIN   KARI KILGORE
DAVID H. HENDRICKSON   JOHANNA ROTHMAN   JOSLYN CHASE
DIANA DEVERELL   JASON A. ADAMS   ANNIE REED

KNOTTED ROAD PRESS

White Collar Crime
Mystery, Crime, and Mayhem: Issue 22
Large Print Edition
Copyright © 2025
All rights reserved

Published 2025 by Knotted Road Press
www.KnottedRoadPress.com

Cover art:
ID 21524694 © Alexander Raths | Dreamstime.com

Cover and Interior design copyright © 2025 Knotted Road Press
www.KnottedRoadPress.com

Never miss an issue of Mystery, Crime, and Mayhem! Get yourself a subscription!

https://www.mysterycrimeandmayhem.com/product/mcm-subscription/

This book is licensed for your personal enjoyment only. All rights reserved. This is a work of fiction. All characters and events portrayed in this book are fictional, and any resemblance to real people or incidents is purely coincidental.
No part of this book may be reproduced in any form or by any electronic or mechanical means, including information storage and retrieval systems, without written permission from the author, except for the use of brief quotations in a book review.

Introduction © 2025 by Leah R Cutter

Essay - Agatha Christie and the Croydon Poisonings © 2025 by Chris Chan

The World's Saddest Party © 2025 by Cate Martin

The Rebirth of a Good Bad Habit © 2025 by Kari Kilgore

The Telltale Scrape © 2025 by David H. Hendrickson

A Classic Case of Misdirection © 2025 by Johanna Rothman

Judge, Jury, and Executioner © 2025 by Joslyn Chase

Dirty Laundry © 2025 by Leah R Cutter

Reckless Endangerment © 2025 by Diana Deverell

That's Not My Daddy—That's an Imposter! © 2025 by Chris Chan

Dirk Knight and the Moving Van Violation © 2025 by Jason A. Adams

Not Dead Yet © 2025 by Annie Reed

CONTENTS

Introduction Leah R Cutter	vii
ESSAY - AGATHA CHRISTIE AND THE CROYDON POISONINGS Chris Chan	1
THE WORLD'S SADDEST PARTY Cate Martin	9
THE REBIRTH OF A GOOD BAD HABIT Kari Kilgore	49
THE TELLTALE SCRAPE David H. Hendrickson	77
A CLASSIC CASE OF MISDIRECTION Johanna Rothman	101
JUDGE, JURY, AND EXECUTIONER Joslyn Chase	119
DIRTY LAUNDRY Leah R Cutter	179

RECKLESS ENDANGERMENT Diana Deverell	219
THAT'S NOT MY DADDY— THAT'S AN IMPOSTER! Chris Chan	239
DIRK KNIGHT AND THE MOVING VAN VIOLATION Jason A. Adams	277
NOT DEAD YET Annie Reed	301
Read More!	355
Our Friends	359

INTRODUCTION
LEAH R CUTTER

When I hear "white collar crime" I'm always reminded of the TV show of the same name, with Matt Bomer. (And it's coming back! The revival was confirmed in June of 2024.)

That show, in some ways, was about the elegance of crime. As well as being a caper show, for the most part. (Capers are generally written from the POV of the "bad guy" and are witty and fun, as well as all about the art of the con and how the bad guy gets away.)

I love capers. As well as the cleverness that some white collar crimes can have.

The stories in this issue may or may not have that elegance. But they do pack a certain punch. I kept reading and shaking my head, knowing that I'd never be able to choose just one favorite from among the fine stories that were placed in my care.

Including the story from our guest author, Johanna Rothman, who knows all about the corporate side of things. You can read more about her on her website at https://www.jrothman.com/

So I have a challenge for you, my dear reader. Could you please pick a favorite, then let me know.

At the end of the year, I have to select stories for awards. Sometimes I select the ones that everyone else loves. Sometimes, I miss.

I truly believe that some of the stories in this issue are award worthy. If you agree with me, please let me know, so I'll pick the ones that the judges would also select.

Because as I said, the stories this issue are so good, I just can't pick a favorite.

Enjoy!
Leah R Cutter
Ravensdale, WA
May 2025

ESSAY – AGATHA CHRISTIE AND THE CROYDON POISONINGS

CHRIS CHAN

True crime is a popular genre, but it has long been controversial, thanks to critics who argue that it can be exploitative. While true crime authors vary widely in the level of respect that they show their subjects, sometimes readers and fans demonstrate a lack of concern for the real-life innocent people whose lives have been turned inside-out due to circumstances outside of their control. Most people never expect to be caught up in a murder, but when it happens, lots of innocent lives are often irreparably damaged.

Christie addressed this theme in her 1958 novel *Ordeal by Innocence.* In it, one character declares, "It's not the guilty that matter. It's the innocent." The plot of *Ordeal by Innocence* centers around a fractured family that thinks it has recovered from the scandal of one member of the family being convicted of the murder of the family matriarch, and later dying in prison. When a witness shows up a couple of years later and proves that the accused man was actually innocent, it throws the family's lives into turmoil, since now they are all under suspicion again and none of them trust each other anymore. These themes were also addressed in detail in Christie's novels *Appointment with Death* and *Ordeal by Innocence*, and her short story "The Four Suspects," just to name a few examples.

Throughout her life, Christie illustrated how murders *needed* to be solved in order to protect the lives and reputations of people who had done no harm. Murderers do not only harm the people they kill. They damage the lives of the living as well.

Christie is not known for writing true crime, but one long-overlooked article was recently recovered and inserted as an appendix in a re-release of The Detection Club's (an association of leading British mystery writers– Christie was the president of the club during the later years of her life) short story collection *Six Against the Yard*. Her article "The Tragic Family of Croydon" was initially published in the August 11, 1929 issue of *The Sunday Chronicle*.

The Croydon Poisonings are unsolved triple homicides that captured the public's attention in England . One by one, three members of the Sydney/Duff family (not hyphened, simply two families connected by marriage) died of arsenic poisoning in 1928 and 1929. Edmund Creighton Duff was a man in his late fifties who died suddenly after fishing on April 27th 1928. The death was initially attributed to sunstroke, and the public was warned to wear hats for protection. Nearly a year later, the forty-year-old Vera Sydney passed away two days after falling ill soon after her midday meal.

Her agonizing death was dismissed as natural stomach trouble. Finally, three weeks after her daughter Vera's death, family matriarch Violet Sydney sickened and swiftly died. Violet blamed tainted medicine, but tests found nothing wrong.

All three were buried quietly, but over the next few weeks, some members of the Sydney/Duff family announced their suspicions, and the women were exhumed and their bodies received a full post-mortem examination. Tests proved they had died from arsenic poisoning, and after Edmund Duff's body was removed from his grave, analysis produced an identical result.

Three deaths from arsenic poisoning had to be murder, or at least two murders and a suicide, as one popular theory claimed that Violet had killed the others and then taken her own life. There was no evidence to back up this conjecture, only the imaginations of a public playing armchair detective. Other suspects included Thomas Sydney, brother of Vera and son of Violet; Edmund Duff's widow Grace, and the Sydney family cook Mrs. Noakes. Motives attributed to them included greed for an inheritance that could fund a new life overseas, an affair with the medical man who performed the initial postmortems, and disgruntled resentment.

None of these theories was ever proven, and

some of these supposed motives may have been based on nothing but pure fancy. In any case, the police never found a satisfactory answer to the crimes, and no one was ever charged. The cloud of suspicion hung over the surviving members of the Sydney/Duff family for the rest of their lives, and some of the suspects lived for over four decades.

Many people theorized about the case, but Christie did not attempt to point a finger of suspicion in "The Tragic Family of Croydon." On the contrary, just as the emotions expressed in her stories illustrated, Christie was less interested in identifying a poisoner than she was in pleading for the public to stop floating theories about the case.

The fairly short article opens with Christie's acknowledgement that the general public has a deep-seated desire to see mysteries solved and justice done. Christie moves on to summarizing the case, its victims, and the other people connected to the case. Raising several unanswered questions as to the motive for the crimes, Christie noted that Edmund Duff's death harmed the financial stability of his entire family.

Christie then moves on to a plea for the public to show mercy for the innocent members of the family and to respect their privacy. Midway through the article, Christie wrote:

"What life has been for them all these three months and what it necessarily must still be is not pleasant to contemplate. They live in a haze of publicity; acquaintances and friends look at them curiously; there are continually autograph hunters, curious idle crowds. Any decent happy private life is made impossible for them.

Add this to any private grief or doubts they may be undergoing and it becomes one of our modern forms of torture which, on the whole, has the Inquisition "beat."

Yet it is unavoidable. The public interest is natural. One would be inhuman did one not feel interested."

Christie closes her essay by writing:

"Let us hope that the truth in the Sydney case will come to light soon and that innocent people be able to take up their lives again free from doubts.

And at the present time let all sympathy and kindly feeling be extended to them in their terrible ordeal."

Since no besides the killer knows for sure who did it, all of the supposed suspects should be given more respect than the gossip mill allows them. Denouncing the anonymous letter-writers who circulated venom and suspicion, Christie asked the public to switch from suspecting the Sydney/Duff family to providing them with moral support while the authorities found the truth.

The culprit responsible for three deaths by arsenic may never be known, but Christie did bring an important reality to the public's attention. It is quite all right to try to pick out the murderer in a work of fiction based on one's imagination. However, real-life people with feelings, reputations, and lives to lead are another matter. There is no justification for adding to the strain felt by the innocent who must live under the cloud of suspicion in a murder case.

THE WORLD'S SADDEST PARTY

CATE MARTIN

Nate Guffman ran into people a lot. It was nearly a daily occurrence for him. Whenever he emerged from the converted storage room that was now the IT department, he would always end up colliding shoulders with someone rushing down the middle of the hallway, or dashing out of an office with armloads of binders and apparently no peripheral vision.

His work buddy Elena had told him this was usually his fault, and Nate guessed she was probably right. Or, at least, it was easier just to agree with her. Yes, he'd probably been looking at the tablet in his hand or even just his own feet. Yes, if he'd been paying attention, he would've heard them coming before running into them. If he was quick enough to agree, she wouldn't explain all over again why her nickname for him was "Fog of War." Then she'd let him get back to focusing on his work and not the rest of the world.

But this day was exceptional somehow. Because first, when he finally left the growing rows of PCs that needed to be wiped and restored to factory settings behind to answer Elena's seventh text summoning him downstairs, he didn't collide with anybody in the hall outside the door. Or further down the hall, as he headed towards the stairs down to the lobby. Despite it only being four in the afternoon, there was no one around for him to run into at all. Which was odd.

Then he reached the security door at the end of the hall. He could see the office cleaner outside with her cart through the glass pane that framed the door, struggling to get her card key out of her jumpsuit pocket. He could see the top of it, cut to be wearable on a lanyard. He knew it was her, although he couldn't exactly remember her name.

But it didn't matter; with the card key, she had access to the offices. He could help her without breaching security. He jogged the last few steps to open the door for her.

And heard a feminine cry of alarm just before the loud crack of metal door meeting human flesh. But she'd been nowhere near the door. He'd seen.

He'd been paying attention.

The heavy door started to swing shut again, muffling a torrent of Spanish. Nate caught it before it could latch, then opened it more slowly this time. The cleaner was still talking. Nate didn't speak much Spanish, and he wasn't the best judge of tone even in English, but he guessed what he was hearing was really a bunch of questions. And someone else was answering them, also in Spanish.

Then he saw the woman he had struck with the door, and for the first time in his life, he felt pretty confident that if asked, he could pick her out of a lineup. A skill Elena insisted he didn't have; that as much as he harped on everyone about following security protocols, anyone wearing the right nametag could get past him without him giving them a second glance.

And it wasn't just the fact that she was wearing the strangest mashup of clothing: a red miniskirt with fluffy white faux-fur trim and tights decorated with sparkling snowflakes, but with a black Victorian era coat and top hat that brought Charles Dickens to mind, and for whatever reason a pair of black paratrooper jump boots. She was also quite tall. Without the top hat, she was probably still over six feet. And her hair was a riot of curls, mostly blonde, but a few locks dyed green and red, presumably for the season.

Then something she said finally got the cleaner to stop fussing over the elbow they were both cradling, and she looked up at Nate hovering in the doorway, which he absolutely wasn't supposed to do. And she smiled at him, a smile that lit up her whole face and danced in her dark green eyes.

"It's fine," she said to him, then repeated it in Spanish to the cleaner. "That door just took me by surprise. I'm not really hurt."

"Sorry," Nate said. He could kind of hear Elena's voice in the back of his head, telling him that he should've said that much sooner. But the woman didn't seem to mind. She just kicked that smile up a couple of more notches.

"Don't worry about it. I should've been standing back, anyway," she assured him.

The cleaner said something Nate didn't catch, but from her gestures, he guessed she needed to get past him with her cart. He stepped out of the way, holding the door for her to get the cart through. She thanked him in English and hustled towards the break room to start her work there.

The woman moved to follow her, but Nate quickly blocked her way before closing the door. "You need to use your card key. For the security logs. It's in the employee handbook."

"Oh, sure," she said, nodding. Then she flashed him a different sort of smile, but not one he could read. "Here's the thing. I don't actually work here?"

"So why are you here?" he asked.

"I'm here for the party," she said. Her voice rose ever so slightly at the end of the sentence, like it was half a statement and half a question.

Nate puzzled that out for a moment, then decided she was making it sound like a question because he was missing social cues again, and she wasn't sure if he was honestly clueless or giving her a hard time on purpose.

"The party," he said. And then he remembered. *That* was why Elena kept texting him. He thought she was just trying to make him change the toner in the printer again because her clothes were nicer than his, even though they were supposed to share that job. He had totally forgotten about the office holiday party.

Well, that explained the empty hallways.

And might explain this woman's costume. Although he still had some questions about that.

"Yeah. I'm Troy's date," she said. And hit him with that smile again.

He wasn't a hundred percent sure, but he thought she might've paused ever so slightly before saying that name. Or was it a question again?

As usual, having a conversation with a stranger was a struggle. But, unlike usual, this one wasn't making him feel exhausted from the effort. He wouldn't mind talking to her longer. He didn't know what all of her smiles meant, but he liked the variety she was directing at him.

However, it was his turn to talk, and he had nothing.

"I don't know Troy," he decided to say. Although he was pretty sure there *was* a Troy.

"That's all right, don't worry about it. I just needed a restroom," she said. She did a little dance and looked longingly at the door behind him.

"There are restrooms downstairs," he said. "They're supposed to be marked when we have events. They're just behind the reception desk."

"Oh, sure," she said. She was quiet for a moment, but if she hoped that Nate would pick up any nonverbal cues from her face or body language…well, then she didn't know Nate.

In the end, she just nodded with a dry laugh that he was pretty sure wasn't directed at him, then gave him a little wave before running down the stairs. She was surprisingly light on her feet, given her choice of footwear. Nate went to the balcony railing to look down into the lobby, but she didn't look back up at him. He watched her curls bounce as her head turned to the left, then the right, before disappearing behind the door that sported a paper cutout of what he guessed was meant to be a lady snowman.

Snow-woman?

Whatever.

Then Elena's voice was in his head again, chiding him for not remembering to even ask for the woman's name. Or giving her his.

THE WORLD'S SADDEST PARTY

And for once, he honestly wished Elena had been there to coach him.

After double-checking that the door behind him was latched, he went down the stairs himself, following the smells of cinnamon and caramelized sugar to the open lobby behind the reception area.

The walls were festooned in silver and blue bunting, and paper cutout snowflakes generously coated in glitter hung from the ceiling. Instrumental holiday music was piping in over the loudspeakers, and most of the light was coming from a quartet of Christmas trees that stood in the corners of the space. Despite the emptiness of the office upstairs, there didn't seem to be many people at the party yet, so Nate didn't feel so bad for being late. He looked around first for something to eat. He could smell cookies, stronger now than when he had first sensed them from the reception desk, but there was supposed to be a dinner thing first. He was hoping for Swedish meatballs and cocktail sausages, like last year. Those had been really good, and no one had minded when he had taken a third helping.

He saw card tables near the trees, covered in silver plastic tablecloths and decked with platters of cheese and cold cuts and baskets of pre-sliced and pre-buttered buns. Not as good as warm food, but he was too hungry to care much. He filled up a plate, occasionally looking around to see if anyone was shooting judgy looks his way. However, everyone was standing in tight little clusters, whispering together.

Or so it seemed to him. He decided the whispers probably weren't about him. He added a few pickles and olives from the relish tray, then finally looked around the room for anyone he recognized.

Well, for Elena. She was honestly the only person who would notice if he was there or not. And she would really notice. If he pulled out a phone, the odds were good he had four more texts from her demanding that he come down. But she was hard to pick out of a crowd, being one of the shortest people he knew.

One of the clusters in the far corner of the room broke up, and he finally saw Elena's dark brown bobbed hair pulled back in a headband that had reindeer antlers on it. She saw him at the same moment he saw her, and she crossed the room to him. Bells hung from the points of her reindeer antlers, and they jingled as she walked. For some reason, this seemed to annoy her, and she tore it off her head as she approached him. She ran a hand through her hair as she glanced at the plate of food in his hands.

But she said nothing. Which scared Nate.

Something was very wrong. And he was missing the clues.

Again.

Bree Taylor stood in front of the bathroom mirror, straightening her top hat and trying to decide what to do next.

She had gotten this far on impulse alone, letting indignant anger drive her across town and into an office building she hadn't been in since she was thirteen. The last time she had come in with her dad on Take Your Daughter To Work Day. It felt like a lifetime ago.

However, everything looked exactly like she remembered it. She was pretty sure the decorations in the party area of the lobby were the same as they had been back then. The snowflakes were holding up surprisingly well. The caked layers of glitter must be protectively thick.

The trees were starting to look a little sad. But maybe that was just the atmosphere in the room. Bree had never been to a more miserable party in her life, and she had barely breezed through it before heading up the stairs.

She had almost gotten all the way there, more easily than she would've thought. The employees at the office party were so caught up in their own drama, no one questioned her presence among them. And then she had arrived at the security door between the public area and the offices, what should have been the end of the road for her, if not for the serendipitous arrival of the office cleaner at nearly the same moment.

A few minutes of chitchat about the party (Juana hadn't known why everyone was so subdued), whether or not the snow expected to fall this evening was going to be as bad as the newscasters said (Juana thought it was, which was why she was cleaning earlier in the afternoon, hoping to avoid driving through a storm), and how annoying it was when dresses didn't come with pockets.

Which was how Bree had come to leave her card key on her desk in her office. And could Juana let her in?

It had been a gamble. If Juana knew employees on sight, she'd know Bree was lying.

But speaking Juana's native language had bought her a little empathy.

She had been so close to getting inside. Then that man had appeared out of nowhere, slammed the door handle right into her funny bone, and then blocked her from her quest.

Not that she was mad about that. In a way, she was kind of glad it had worked out that way. He hadn't let her inside, which was frustrating, and he hadn't been swayed by her most winning charms. Even in this ridiculous dress her sister had convinced her to wear, which hadn't been the costume she had wanted at all. She had nothing but her own lack of planning ahead to blame for that.

Mostly she was glad because his words about logging the card keys made her very aware that if she got caught inside the offices, Juana would likely be blamed and fired for letting her in. And, as much as she didn't plan to get caught, she didn't want to risk someone else's livelihood on her quest.

But also because that man had been the most intriguing guy she'd met in months. He listened to her so intently, like every word she uttered was full of meaning he was eager to discern. And he hadn't leered at the dress she had let her sister talk her into wearing, although she wouldn't have blamed him if he had. It was that kind of dress.

No, he had mostly been focusing on her boots. Her Corcoran jump boots. They were her favorite things in the world; she wore them everywhere. He had studied them pretty intently, but hadn't asked about them, to her disappointment.

And he had sneaked little looks up at her, like he was trying to read her face, but didn't want to gaze on it too long all at once. It was awkward and charming. And probably for the best. Bree didn't like her chances resisting those chocolate brown eyes if they had lingered on hers for more than those brief flashes.

He hadn't mentioned his name, but he was definitely too young to remember her coming in with her dad. And she was pretty sure he was in IT, not sales. Sales people tended to not wear button-up shirts with patterns from *JoJo's Bizarre Adventure* on them. Purple and gold at a Christmas party. Bold choice. She liked it.

However, she wasn't here to meet a guy. She was here for her dad.

So, everything in the building was the same. That meant the CEO's office would be in the same place, in the midpoint of that endless corridor of offices beyond the security door she had completely failed to bluff her way past. The office that had belonged to jolly, old Hank McCormick back in the day. He had always had a bowl full of M&M's on his desk and would fill an entire Dixie cup with them for Bree to snack on when she was there.

Now, that office belonged to Dave Uhlstrom. And Dave never shared. She doubted he even liked sweets. Greed and bitterness, that summed up Dave Uhlstrom.

And he was in charge now. He had been for the last few years. So his being the boss didn't explain the oppressive atmosphere at the company party.

No, something new had happened. Something someone had interrupted her family's game night to call her father about.

He hadn't explained what the call was about, but Bree had overheard the crucial letters SDI. The company her father had walked away from years before. Whatever he had heard had brought that same wounded look to his eyes that she remembered from the day he'd come home with all of his work things in a banker's box. Like he'd been stabbed in the back.

She didn't know what had inflicted this wound, but she knew well why he had walked away without any compensation from the company he had helped build from a startup.

And, while she couldn't do anything to fix any of that and she knew it, there was something she *could* do.

She could get her father the perfect Christmas gift. Because while she knew there was certainly no bowl of free-for-the-taking M&M's in Dave Uhlstrom's office, there was something else in there. Something that she felt completely free to take, because it never should've been his in the first place.

Bree adjusted her borrowed outfit, fluffed her curls back out of her face, then headed back out into the miserable party.

Maybe she could find a guy named Troy and convince him to be her cover.

But if she ended up face to face with a certain nameless man in a JoJo shirt, she'd be sure to get his name this time.

Nate put the last of a turkey sandwich in his mouth and chewed. Then he licked a bit of mustard off the side of his thumb. He found his plastic cup of lemon-lime soda and took a long drink. But he knew that was as long as he could successfully stall Elena.

"What were the clues again?" he finally asked. "I mean, I know you told me to look around. All I see is that it's cold food this year, not like last year. But I guess that's not it."

"Actually, Fog of War, the food is part of it," she

said. Then she blew out a tired sigh and muttered, "The food is always part of it."

"Part of what?" he asked. This conversation was tiring. He turned to look towards the food table. But also to scan the room again. Had that woman just left the party? Or was she still in the restroom? Unlike Elena, he knew he'd spot her in any crowd. Tall, and in a top hat to boot, she couldn't possibly hide.

"That's right, you weren't here in 2017," Elena said.

"2017," Nate repeated. Then something clicked. "That's when they stopped giving out end of the year bonuses for employees. Because there were shareholders who needed the money." That had been six months before he had started, but everyone had still been sore about it. Since the founding of the company, profit sharing with the employees had meant merry Christmases all around. But that had been before Nate's time.

"We had a potluck," Elena told him. "We all brought in a dish to share. And then Uhlstrom told us all that he was cancelling Christmas."

"I don't think that's how he put it," Nate said. He had more to say, but a flash of red in the corner of his vision drew his attention away from Elena and his ham sandwich both. He turned his head just in time to catch that bright smile. But it was aimed at someone else.

Was that Troy?

He still wasn't sure if there *was* a Troy.

"Listen, before you try defending him," Elena said, but her voice was lower now, and he had to both move closer and hunker down a little to hear her words, "I know you're not good at reading a room, and that's fine. But you are good at your job. You must've worked out why so many PCs and laptops got turned in today."

"I don't know. Most of them didn't have a ticket opened in the company-wide system," Nate said. "The employees are supposed to do that before they dump them in our office. I guess it's a holiday thing?"

"Everyone wants all of their data wiped from the company computers to start fresh in the new year?" Elena asked him.

"You're being sarcastic," he said.

"Well spotted, Fog of War," Elena said. "Look around the room for me. Notice people. Besides that woman in the top hat you keep looking at, I mean. She doesn't even work here."

"Who is she?" Nate asked.

"Tall and blonde? Probably someone's date. Would you focus?"

"Who's Troy?" Nate asked.

"Oh my god, focus!" Elena said, grabbing his arms and shaking him with a bit more force than he would've expected.

"You're mad," he said, and took a step back from her.

"Yeah, but not at you," she said. But she was visibly calming down now. "Listen. Our fearless leader, the one who had us all throw our own party to celebrate our freedom from holiday bonuses, is now hosting a bash for we few, we lucky few, who still have jobs."

She had spaced out those last four words, almost making them four separate sentences. Nate chewed on a bite of sandwich while he put that together in his head. Then he looked around the room again.

And finally noticed how few people were there. And no one was upstairs; everyone in the building had come down. Only there were less than half the number of people who should've been there.

Then he looked at the tables of food. Cold cuts, cheese and buns to make sandwiches. But only enough for half of last year's crowd.

Whoever had put the catering order in had known ahead of time that their numbers would be reduced. Had it been Dave Uhlstrom himself? Or had his assistant done it? And lived with the secret for how many days?

Unless it hadn't really been a secret.

"Did you know this was happening?" Nate asked Elena.

"No," she said, and brushed something off her face. "No, for once, you weren't the only one left in the dark. And now we're all just standing here, too numb to go home yet. But you're the only one actually eating, Nate."

It was rare for Elena to use his first name. It meant something, but he wasn't sure what. He hoped it was something good. He much preferred to be called Nate than to be called Fog of War. He didn't get *that* focused on his work.

Elena brushed at her face again, almost angrily, like something was annoying her. But it was the wrong time of year for mosquitos.

Another flash of red caught his eye, and he glanced over to see that woman in the Dickens coat and top hat skipping silently back up the stairs to the offices above.

"Oh, I see why you were asking about Troy," Elena said with a sniff. "Yeah, that woman you've been watching was standing next to him. I guess she's his date? Frankly, she looks too interesting for a guy like Troy, but maybe it's a first date or something. Hey, what are you doing?"

That last she squeaked out as Nate thrust his plate with two uneaten sandwiches still on it into her hands. She had to grab it from him just to keep it from smashing into the front of her Argyle sweater vest.

"I have to get back upstairs," he said.

He supposed it was ironic, but he was really hoping that she would know what he meant without him saying it. That she would take the hint.

But when she grinned up at him, he knew she had. "I think I'll go chat with Troy over there," she said with a wink.

He didn't quite know what that wink meant, but he knew from the words that Elena was going to do her best to keep Troy from wondering where his date had gone.

Not that Nate could focus on anything else. Half of his coworkers had just been laid off, and he wasn't sure what that meant for the rest of them. Pay cuts? Part-time hours? Change to benefits?

But he didn't care about any of that so much as he desperately needed to know who the woman in the top hat was.

And what she wanted so badly on the other side of the security door.

Unlike her nameless IT guy, Troy had been *exactly* like all the guys she had been meeting since college.

And to think her family kept asking her why she didn't date more.

But it didn't matter. She had gotten what she had been after: Troy's key card. She didn't even need to follow through on her impulsive plan to try picking it out of his pocket. As it turned out, when she had asked to use it to go to the restroom, he had just given it to her. If he knew about the public rooms behind the reception desk, he hadn't brought it up.

He had offered to accompany her, half-heartedly implying that she might not feel safe in the empty, dark offices, but not bothering to disguise his real thoughts much. But she had given him her brightest smile and slipped away from his grasping hands with promises to be right back.

Whatever, she had done it. She had gotten inside.

There was no sign of Juana. Perhaps she was already on her way home to her family, beating the snow that the notifications on Bree's phone was still promising would be epic.

There was no sign of anybody else, either. No couples slipping away from the party downstairs for a private moment. No drunk people clustered around the copier.

Bree had never worked in an office. She freely admitted her ideas of what happened inside them were likely based on too many movies and not enough lived experience.

But whatever, it was unsettling how quiet it was. And when she passed the open doors of darkened offices, she could see signs of disarray. If she had made it inside on her first attempt, she might have found those clues puzzling. But after a few minutes at the World's Saddest Party, she had the big picture now. She knew what had put that look on her father's face at dinner.

The company he had put so much sweat equity into all through her childhood, he had never stopped loving the people it represented to him. Not even after he'd chosen to walk away.

And now it was all falling apart. His mentor had chosen to put the reins into the hands of the likes of Dave Uhlstrom, and Dave had only taken a few years to run it all into the ground.

Half of the company had just been laid off on

the day of the holiday party. Christmas was just a few days away. How many families had just had their holidays ruined by sudden unemployment and so much uncertainty about the future?

Anyway, that explained the World's Saddest Party. And the offices that had recently had all personal effects yanked out of them in a hurry.

Suddenly, what she was here to do felt kind of small.

But it really wasn't. She was only here to steal a symbol, true enough. But if what it symbolized had been respected, all of these people's lives would be very different today. She knew that as deeply as she knew anything.

She found the CEO's office just as surely as she had known she would.

Of course, Troy's key card only brought a red light of warning when she tapped it against the mechanism.

Well, that had always been a longshot. His key card had gotten her through the main door, and that had been enough. Without even a momentary hint of remorse, she stuffed the key card into the nearest trash can.

Then she ducked into the office next to the CEO's. She didn't know whose office this was, but it must be someone important's, since family photos and plastic knick-knacks were still scattered around the desk. *Someone* still had a job.

She put her hands on the corners of that desk, braced her booted feet firmly on the carpet tiled floor, and shoved with all her might.

Nate tapped his card, opened the door, and stepped into the dark of the hallway just in time to hear a loud, resonating boom. Not a sound he could place. Then there was a rasping sound he couldn't identify either, but he was on the move anyway, heading down the long hallway to where the sounds seemed to be coming from.

The grunt of effort was confusing, as it seemed to be coming from a point higher up than even a six-foot tall woman should be.

He almost walked right past it, but this time it wasn't a flash of red that caught his eye. No, all that red was already out of sight when he skidded to a stop in the doorway of the CFO's office.

There, up by the ceiling, the low safety lights were reflecting off the glitter on a pair of snowflake-covered tights, and the shine on a spit-polished pair of jump boots.

No, not *by* the ceiling. *In* the ceiling.

That woman had pushed the desk against the wall, shifted aside a couple of ceiling tiles, and was in the process of hoisting herself over the wall that divided the two offices.

But any comparison his mind might want to make between her and a cat burglar was undercut considerably by the difficulty she was having with the maneuver. In fact, it looked like she had gotten caught halfway.

"Do you need some help?" he called up from in front of the desk.

"Why? Are you offering?" she called back down.

There was a muffled sound that sounded like some artful swearing, but her head was on the other side of the wall, so he wasn't sure he caught the exact words.

Then she must have turned to toss over her shoulder, "I think I've got it, thanks. I want to say I'm regretting letting my sister talk me into dressing up like Elizabeth Banks from *Fred Claus* when *I* wanted to dress up as Cindy Lou Who, but I never would've made it even this far with a mermaid train nightdress on."

Then she laughed. And Nate felt little electric shivers all up and down his spine.

"I've not seen *Fred Claus*," he said, "but I quite liked her as Wyldstyle in *The Lego Movie*."

Which was probably the dumbest thing to say ever, and he regretted it. For about half a second. Then he heard her laugh again, and the shivers were back.

"I *loved* that character!" she said, swinging her booted feet in a way that very effectively communicated her joy. "It's the only way my sister talked me into this dress. And, hey! I like your shirt."

"Thanks. I'm told it's very purple." He didn't add that he suspected that wasn't meant as a compliment.

"It's a JoJo pattern, right?" she said.

"Yeah," he said, dumbstruck. "I've had this shirt for five years. No one has ever known what it was before."

"It's subtle, you know?" she said. Then her feet kicked again, but this time more for an attempt at climbing momentum than in joy.

It didn't seem to have her desired effect.

"I think I Pooh Beared myself," she said. "Can I take you up on that help now?"

"What do you need me to do?" he asked. He had a sudden horror that she was going to ask him to push her the rest of the way through. From behind. That was not what he had been offering at all.

But she said, "I think what I need is a hand from the other side here. Is that remotely possible?"

"You know that's the CEO's office, right?" Nate said.

"I do," she admitted.

"Yeah. I guess that's why you're trying to get into it."

He had never felt so conflicted in his life. The urge to help her was strong. But violating security protocols? To break into the boss's office?

That wasn't him at all.

She must have heard something in his words or in his silence, because when she spoke again, the merry laughter was all gone from her voice.

"Listen…what's your name?"

He felt like slapping his own forehead. He had messed up introductions a second time. "Nate. Nate Guffman," he said.

"Hello, Nate Guffman. I'm Bree Taylor. Does that name mean anything to you?"

"You don't work here," he said. Because he would remember a first name like Bree for sure. It was a village in Middle Earth, just to start with.

"Yeah, but my dad was one of the founders, back in the day," she said. "Phil Taylor?"

"Sorry, I think that was before my time," he said.

"That's okay," she said. "Look, I'm not here to do any industrial espionage or bust into any safes or anything. But Dave Uhlstrom has something in his office that really belongs to my dad. And I was kind of hoping I could get it for him. Tonight."

"I don't think he's even here," Nate said, running back his memory of the party downstairs. No, the boss hadn't been there. Just shell-shocked employees in muttering clumps.

"No, dropping a bomb on everyone's lives then not bothering to show his face is very Dave Uhlstrom," she said. Then she kicked her feet again. "I think I'm starting to lose blood flow to my feet. If you can't—or won't—help me out, that's cool. But can you at least help me down?"

Nate tried to remember any interaction he had ever had with Dave Uhlstrom. He couldn't summon a single one, beyond seeing him speak at company-wide events. Nate didn't usually think about whether he liked people or not. They were just people. Always there. He knew he wasn't supposed to think of them as *interchangeable*, but sometimes, to him, they just were. If Dave Uhlstrom wasn't his boss, someone else would fill that role. Would anything much change?

He wanted to say no, but then he remembered

the way Elena had been brushing at her face while talking about Uhlstrom cancelling Christmas.

Oh. Right. She had been fighting back tears. Because Elena would never cry at work. She had told him so herself.

Except she kind of had been. Because of their boss.

"Nate?" Bree called from up in the ceiling.

"Sorry. I can help," he said.

"Great! I'm going to try shifting my hips back. I just need you to kind of catch me if I fall. I think both my legs have gone to sleep," she said.

"No, I meant, I can help you get into that office."

And then he went out into the hall and over to the CEO's door. He might never have met his boss, but he knew a few things about him just from providing him with security measures over the years.

Security measures he didn't like taking. Like remembering to carry a key card. Which was why his door had a number pad backup.

And like remembering a unique PIN. Which was why Nate was willing to bet the PIN that opened the door was Dave Uhlstrom's birthdate.

It took longer to find that on the company's Good News page from back in October when his birthday had been on the 20th than it did to get inside the office once he had it.

Nate wondered why he didn't just prop the door open with a trashcan when he was out. It would be almost as secure.

He went inside the office, closing the door behind him before switching on the lights. And saw a head framed in blonde, red and green curls under a slightly askew top hat emerging from the gap where a ceiling tile had once been.

It took him a minute to realize the reason his face felt so strange was that when she smiled down on him with such utter delight; he was grinning back up at her. When was the last time he had used those muscles?

But somehow, he just couldn't stop.

Bree wasn't exactly sure how getting out of the ceiling was going to work. She imagined it was going to be exactly like it had been for Pooh Bear, with a lot of tugging followed by a tumble to the floor that was bound to hurt.

But Nate had a plan in mind, clearly. He pushed the desk over to the wall, mirroring what she had done on the other side. Then he put the ottoman from the Eames chair that stood in the corner of the room on top of the desk. When he climbed on top of both of those, he was high enough up to support her. She put her hands on his shoulders and leveraged her back half through the Great Tightness until she was more or less in his arms.

Which was nice. However, he put her down right away. Which was a disappointment. But, as she reminded herself for the umpteenth time, she wasn't here to find a guy.

"We should get down. This isn't particularly stable," he said.

"Right," she said, and carefully stepped from the top of the ottoman to the desktop, then into the seat of the office chair, then down onto the floor.

She wouldn't pretend to care that she left prominent boot prints of white ceiling tile dust on each of those surfaces. Or bother trying to wipe them clean.

"What are we looking for?" Nate asked as he jumped lightly down from the desk, then put the ottoman back to where he had found it.

He didn't wipe it clean either, Bree noticed. But she turned her attention to the shelves that stood behind the usual position of the desk. The shelves that would appear behind him in videoconferences. The brag shelves.

And there it was, in the total point of pride. The plaque that really should have been her father's. She picked it up reverently, pulling the sleeve of her coat down over her hand to use it to polish the brass.

Not that it needed it. The words were clear for all to see. SALES PERSON OF THE DECADE.

Nate moved to stand behind her and read that plaque over her shoulder. He didn't say anything at first, but she was getting used to that with him. He considered what he wanted to say before he said it. She found that quality charming as all get out.

"This was your father's?" he said.

"It was supposed to be," Bree said softly. "He earned it. But Dave lied. Dave lied *a lot*. My dad, he's a great guy. He's as honest as the day is long. And we can skip any jokes about sales people, okay?"

"I wasn't going to make any," Nate said.

"Yeah, I know," she said. "The problem with my dad is, he thinks everyone else is as honest as he is. He had no idea how many of his accounts were being credited to Dave Uhlstrom. Like, Uhlstrom was stealing the commissions and the credit and *everything*. And when my dad found out, he went to the big boss at the time. Hank McCormick. I used to think Hank was a great guy, too. But even with all the evidence my dad gave him about what was happening, he still believed Dave Uhlstrom. Or, maybe not believed exactly, but decided he needed someone like Uhlstrom more than he needed someone like my dad. I don't know. I just know that there was a big party, and Dave Uhlstrom got this plaque and a big promotion that eventually led to him running this place. Into the ground, but whatever."

"And your dad?" Nate asked.

"My dad never worked in sales again," she said. "He was really good at it. And he loved the work. But he walked away and never came back." She clutched the plaque tightly in her hands, enough to make her fingertips turn white. "This is his. And I'm going to give it to him. I don't know if he's even going to want it, to be honest. But *I* want him to have it."

Then she finally did what her father would've wanted her to do in the first place. She took a deep breath, and let all the anger go.

"So, what do you think?" she asked Nate. And weirdly, she felt shy about it. She had no idea how much he had seen of her back end when she'd been stuck in between the two offices, but this was the moment where she felt the awkwardness.

And there was another long silence as he thought it over. She watched his brown eyes moving over the letters on the plaque like he was reading it again, character by character. Then he looked up at her, the longest bit of eye contact they'd had yet.

Yeah, she had been right about those eyes. They were definitely going to be her undoing. Whatever he said next, she already knew she was going to find herself agreeing to it. Even if he told her to turn herself in as a wannabe thief on Christmas.

But then he licked his lips, still considering his words, before saying, "I think we should get this plaque to your dad."

"Yeah?" she said, and he nodded. But she wasn't sure he understood what she was asking him. So she added, "We?"

"Oh," he said, and looked away from her in sudden confusion.

"I mean, you helped out. I would love for you to be there when I give it to him."

He said nothing, so she pressed on. "If you want."

He still didn't speak or even look at her. So the conversational ball bounced back into her court. "I understand if you're busy, you know. The party and all."

He finally looked up at her again, but with deep confusion in his eyes. "Party?"

"There's a party going on downstairs right now. I mean, I keep calling it the World's Saddest Party in my head, but that's probably just me being snarky."

"It *is* the World's Saddest Party," he said. And then he was grinning at her again. "I don't really like parties in the first place, but that title really fits, doesn't it?"

"It does," she said. Then she tucked the plaque close to her side with one arm, then looped the other through his so they could walk together. Out of this office, out of this building, out of this cursed company.

However, they had to pass the remains of that party first. Bree was willing to linger if he had any goodbyes to say first, but he only scanned the room until he found a short woman with dark brown bobbed hair standing next to Troy. Bree could tell just from her body language that this woman was thoroughly fed up with Troy's company. At the sight of Nate leaving the building, she only gave him a little wave of acknowledgement.

When Nate had looked away, she gave Bree an exuberant double thumbs-up. She just managed not to laugh out loud. She didn't know who that woman was, but she was clearly a friend of Nate's. And she had just gotten Nate's friend's seal of approval.

"What's that?" Nate said, distracted.

"I was just wondering what you planned to do now," Bree said, sliding closer to Nate's side as they stepped out into the cold, yet still snow-free, night.

"We were going to your dad's?" he said uncertainly.

"I meant career-wise. I guess you didn't get laid off since you're still here. Are you planning to hang on until the bitter end, or on to new pastures?"

"Oh. I hadn't thought about it," he said. "If I get fired for helping you rob the boss's office, I guess it's a moot point."

"Please. We got away scot-free," she said. "But if you ask my dad, he'll tell you that walking away from that company was the best decision of his life."

"I thought you were upset about it?"

"I mean, yeah. And he was too, at the time. And I still think he could get back into sales anytime he wanted to."

Nate thought that over, then asked, "What *does* he do now?"

"At the moment? He travels around the state to

elementary schools and dresses up like Charles Dickens to read them stories. This time of year, it's *A Christmas Carol*, of course," she said, and put her hand on her top hat.

"Oh!" he said, flushing red again. "I thought that was part of the *Fred Claus* thing."

"What?" she laughed.

"I've never seen the movie," he said.

"Okay, fair enough," she said, and unlocked the passenger door of her car to let him inside. But she paused before stepping out of the way to look at him again. "Were you thinking the same thing about my boots?"

"Your boots?" he said, looking down at them again. Then he looked up at her, and even in the flickering light from the parking lot pole behind her, those eyes gave her a little jolt again.

"My boots. Not what she wore in the movie. Or Dickens either, if I have to point that out," she said.

"I mean, they're just you, right?" He glanced down at the boots, then up at her again. "Yeah. They're like part of you."

"They are," Bree agreed, then to both of their surprise, she kissed him on the cheek.

She circled around the car to get in on the driver's side and got inside. She could feel Nate watching her, but he didn't speak until she had gotten the engine running and was turning up the heat.

"You know, Elena says I'm not very good with people," he said.

"Does she?" Bree said. She supposed that would be true, both that Elena had told him so as well as the words themselves.

"I guess I thought that was something you should know. You know. Like, now?"

He sounded like he'd left nervous behind a couple of exits back and was on the road to petrified now. She turned in her seat to smile at him her warmest smile. "I'm not people, though. I'm Bree. And I think you're turning out to be pretty good with Bree. Don't you think?"

And, for the second time that night, she teased a grin out of him. The fact that it was so unpracticed a gesture on his face made it all the more charming in her mind.

"Well, I guess we'll see," he said.

"We'll see," she agreed. Then she thrust the plaque into his hands so she could put her car into reverse and get them as far away from the remains of Dave Uhlstrom's company as fast as they could.

THE REBIRTH OF A GOOD BAD HABIT

KARI KILGORE

The thing about old habits, especially bad ones, wasn't that they died hard. Not in Suzanne Everhart's fifty-three years of living on Planet Earth, anyway.

The thing was those habits didn't die at all, no matter how long you spent trying to ignore them.

Take the simplest, most ordinary task she'd performed about a thousand times in her role as a stable, reliable, upstanding member of her Decatur, Georgia, community. Attending the opening of yet another dedication of some sort of statue or plaque or park bench or whatever else the local Committee for Keeping the Wealthy Folks Busy and Socially Engaged came up with.

Suzanne kept waiting for the newest crop of busybodies to switch to presenting the honorees with an eco-friendly gold-plated compost bucket or ceremonial precious-crystal "Wine O'Clock" glass or maybe even a set of cloth diapers made from imported hand-brushed limited-edition ultra-organic bamboo/hemp hybrid.

Perhaps she needed to switch to decaf after two in the afternoon.

But for now, she clutched her stainless-steel coffee mug a little tighter (engraved with the clever logo from a local shop rather than a corporate chain, of *course*), with her well-practiced I'm-friendly-but-not-interested-in-chatting smile firmly in place.

She and her fellow Pillars of Progressive Society had gathered together on a refreshingly cool April afternoon on the perfectly groomed lawn of one of their most active and moneyed members.

The near-constant roar of Friday afternoon Atlanta traffic would not *dare* intrude upon such a rarified atmosphere. And the thick, squared-off row of precisely trimmed silvery green hedges served as an insurance policy.

The refined, gentle splashing of several angular Art Deco-style granite fountains just inside the hedge filled in the sonic gaps.

Ms. Chanelle McGill-Candler had taken great pains to transform the outer edges of the generous property's party space away from the water and fertilizer and pesticide-intensive roses, exotics, and fancy flowers her family had preferred for decades.

An effort Suzanne approved of all the way down to the bottom of her own sensible and waste-hating Midwestern roots. Something about the Atlanta area's obsession with an unnaturally green lawn no matter the consequences—including programming hidden sprinklers to water in the middle of the night during drought restrictions—turned her stomach.

So with the exception of the deeply green and velvety golf-course look obviously preserved for such occasions, the borders of McGill-Candler held clumps of taller, browner grasses, low scrubby bushes, and perfectly lovely flowers Suzanne thought looked better than overly fussy roses anyway.

The high, cloyingly sweet perfume of rare or hybrid blooms that too often floated through these sorts of yards would have been far too much on top of the thick aromas of high-end cologne and perfume she could just about *see* in the air.

The part of the house she could see from her preferred spot on the outside edge of the crowd was a sand-colored stone model, probably built in the 1970s in a high-dollar effort to look much older barely fifty years later. Her gaze kept straying from Ms. Chanelle McGill-Candler and her endless speechifying to the graceful picture windows overlooking this surviving patch of overly coddled grass, then to the generous sliding glass doors that opened into the basement "entertainment wing."

Complete with a twenty-seat cinema-style home theater equipped with the latest projection and sound and ultra-fast streaming technology, if the rumors were to be believed.

Rumors about openly conspicuous consumer

sorts like Chanelle were almost always safe grounds for belief.

No matter how many acres of the vast family estate she re-purposed for native landscaping, or how many absurdly expensive awards she sponsored for *other* people's hard work to address stubborn inequality that lingered in their just-east-of-Atlanta neighborhood.

Like the silver gardening spade she presented right now to a group of high school kids who'd given up their whole winter and spring breaks to help set up garden boxes in some of Decatur's lowest-income communities.

To their ever-increasing credit, the group of boys and girls who'd shown up dressed up in their usual gardening gear (as requested) more or less managed to keep their expressions grateful and respectful when faced with Chanelle's immaculate cream-colored silk pantsuit and Easter Sunday-appropriate levels of makeup and huge embellished hat. Too many of the women and men standing by waiting to politely applaud and make sure they were visible wore outfits just that expensive, out-of-touch, and likely to make the guests of honor feel like they'd been set up to feel stupid.

Suzanne herself had stayed with her usual wardrobe of charcoal gray pants and matching jacket, with some kind of earthy or jewel tone underneath, with her eternally red waves falling loose past her shoulders to celebrate the rare day of Georgia not trying to sweat her to death.

Exactly what those who'd seen and greeted her at too many of these soirees knew to expect. A habit she'd learned many years ago in her intensive, methodical study of how to fit in no matter the situation. Especially a situation that involved spending time with well-to-do types.

With her former line of work/favorite hobby, standing out simply would not do.

Today that meant a vivid, deep green to actually honor those great kids, which she hoped would help make up for the others. And maybe for the absurd silver spade, when what they really needed was useful equipment and more funding.

Which brought her right back to gazing at those big, expensive windows again.

Wondering whether the security system at this fine, overly moneyed estate was as antiquated as the owner was. Perhaps following the same creaky misconception that while the neighborhood and Atlanta and the world might change all around them, people like Ms. Chanelle McGill-Candler would be just fine preserved in her bubble of wealth and privilege where no trace of modern reality dare intrude.

Suzanne took in a sharp breath when the polite applause finally washed over her, yanking her back from calculations and assessments best left in her own overachieving youth.

At least these kids probably had most of their most impressive accomplishments out in the open, rather than using impressive academics as a cover for their more important, effective activities.

For Suzanne, most of the fun back then stayed decidedly out of sight and almost completely unknown.

Which was a huge part of the reason it *was* so much fun.

She finished the cool remains of her coffee with her normal, rather childish thrill in filling the expensive cup with the same damn Maxwell House her southern Illinois grandparents had sworn by.

At an unexpected touch on her shoulder, Suzanne forced her face not to take on the defensive tension in her body. Whatever her public (and private) reasons for associating with this too-often frivolous crowd, idle socializing beyond the required amounts didn't fit the bill.

Neither did ill-fated attempts to alter her carefully protected single-and-absolutely-*not*-looking status.

But rather than a clueless, chirpy socialite or an

openly ambitious person looking to make her romantic acquaintance, a ghost from her long-gone, much-missed past stood beside her.

A ghost dressed in the same fitting-in-anywhere style, with a lilac skirt that frothed like springtime around her ankles, and a matching blouse with lacy short sleeves. Her short brown hair walked the delicate line between too youthful and too matronly, much like her flirty rose-gold-framed glasses.

A remarkable transformation from a gawky, braces-wearing, utterly goofy girl who needed hours of giggly help with her math homework all through high school.

And Suzanne couldn't pretend she wasn't face-to-face with her best friend and partner in private adventures for a long time, a long time ago.

Leslie McIntyre.

"Quite a production," Leslie said, focusing on the group of young gardeners rather than Suzanne. Leslie had shed the flat, slightly nasal voice stamp of southern Illinois even more than Suzanne. Likely because Leslie had taught her that vocal flexibility. "They're doing a brilliant job acting happy about their *sweet* little trophy, aren't they?"

Suzanne smiled, a more genuine one than she usually managed in the exceedingly rare moments when she was honestly surprised.

"That's an important skill for ambitious young people," she said. "The ability to appear grateful when they're actually wondering who lost the plotline and thought something this ridiculous was a good idea. I often wonder if people who don't learn how before they turn sixteen can ever catch up."

Now Leslie glanced over, with a warm echo of the mischievous smile Suzanne remembered so fondly and so well.

"I've met a few late in life to that particular skill, and they never quite seem to catch up. No matter how talented a teacher they work with. How's it going, Suz?"

Suzanne laughed under her breath at the idea of anyone who traveled in her current circles daring to call her that.

Or anyone else in her life besides the woman standing next to her.

"I'd say I'm empathizing with those poor kids more than I expected to by this stage of my life. What brings you down to the capitol of the New South, Les?"

The group of overdressed and over-privileged adults moved toward the children, eager to offer their dubious wisdom and snap that all-important, "I'm *so* supportive of our compassionate youth" photo for immediate upload to Instagram.

Leaving Suzanne with even more privacy around her than she usually contrived for herself.

"Oh, you know how it is," Leslie said, still watching the gathering in front of them. "Always looking for new ways to hone my craft. I consider myself lucky to have found one I can practice for the rest of my days rather than having to consider the horrors of retirement. I hear it steals so much of the enjoyment and pleasure that make life worth living."

Now, Suzanne's smile was wistful, which was surely an improvement over the pure glaring daggers she would have hurled at anyone else who hit that close to how she'd been feeling lately.

"I've heard the same. I won't say whether I think that's true or not just yet."

Leslie finally turned toward Suzanne with a curious, searching expression in her blue eyes.

Then she tilted her head to the side and away from the oh-so-proper gathering, squinched up her eyes, and stuck out her tongue exactly the way she had as a gangly teenager when the two of them were bored out of their minds.

Suzanne snorted out laughter and immediately covered it with a convincing-enough cough that no one else even glanced their way.

Or maybe everyone else was too caught up in their own importance to notice.

And Suzanne found she didn't give a damn whether they noticed or not when she pulled Leslie into a big hug more than ten years overdue.

"Seriously, how on earth are you here right now?" Suzanne said, blinking back tears. "This isn't exactly the kind of A-list event I'd expect to bring out someone with your peculiar interests and specialized skill set."

"I could say the same of you, couldn't I? Doesn't seem like your kind of crowd, at least not last time we were on speaking terms."

Suzanne shook her head and did her best not to frown.

"It's not that we weren't on speaking terms, and you know it. Our paths just…We went in different directions is all."

Leslie shrugged, then grinned. "Fair enough. Maybe you can tell me more about that sometime instead of up and disappearing on me for a decade or so. As far as my field trip, you know I've always tried to champion young people when I can, especially if they're interested in farming and gardening and such. Something you taught me a long, long time ago when no one else championed me for much of any damn thing at all."

That was how it all started, way back during their first youthful experiments with less-than-legally-acceptable means of leveling the unfairness they found in life. When a spontaneous theft on Suzanne's part made such a difference in her, Leslie's, and all their classmates' high-school-misery levels.

That entirely unplanned success launched the two of them into a long, exciting, entirely planned series of righting wrongs and redressing imbalances that stretched from their early teen years into their late forties.

When the potential consequences got all too painful and real to Suzanne, and she'd decided her sanity and survival were worth more than continuing to chase righteous thrills and satisfaction.

"You were worth championing, Les, and I'm damn sure you still are. Listen, I doubt anyone's going to notice if I disappear now that the absurd main event is over. Nothing left to see but the self-congratulatory canapes that Ms. Chanelle McGill-Candler no doubt had catered at great expense rather than *sourcing* the ingredients from the community garden we're here to celebrate. Want to get out of here?"

Leslie spared one last glance toward the basement sliding glass doors Suzanne had been contemplating herself only a few short minutes ago.

When she returned her intense, unsettling focus, Suzanne wished she hadn't.

"Oh, I don't know. I think this is the most interesting location in the whole Southeast myself. How much do you know about how your gracious hostess and her family came by their immense resources?"

Suzanne held her breath for several seconds, until her head pulsed in time with her heartbeat.

Was she actually going to do this?

Even consider *thinking* about getting involved in her old pursuits, when she'd spent so many years creating careful walls between herself and the memories that wanted nothing more than to seduce her back inside?

"I make a point of not knowing much about people lately," she said. "That's the only way I manage to maintain the social connections and influence I have down here. It may not seem like much to you, or anyone else who knew me a long time ago. But I get more accomplished than you might think from this side of the equation."

"I know you do. I hope you don't mind, but I've been keeping track of what all you've gotten done since we parted company. Mainly to help myself understand why you'd made such a...*surprising* turn in your path, you might say. You've encouraged crowds like this to open their wallets for a hell of a lot of good causes, Suz. More and better than they ever would have without your steady, safe influence."

The group had taken themselves to a sprawling copper-hued tent set up to protect those pricy canapes, apparently without noticing Suzanne's absence. A turn of events she would have welcomed even without Leslie showing up out of nowhere.

"I moved down here with someone I cared a lot about," Suzanne said softly. "After the last gig you and I pulled. From a family that moved in these circles, you might say. She taught me a different kind of game to play when it comes to changing the world for the better. One that doesn't involve the risk of going to prison. Or getting killed."

Leslie kept looking into Suzanne's eyes instead of looking away or even flinching. Showing a lot more courage and loyalty than Suzanne had when one of their own made a fatal mistake in what should have been a lark of a job.

A mistake that drove Suzanne out of the life for good.

At least that's what she'd been telling herself, more and more often over the last several years.

"So you've been making good on your big ambition to change the world," Leslie said, and now her face turned sympathetic. "Changing one person or family or community's world absolutely counts. And anyone who manages that much deserves to be happy about it. I just wonder if you *can* be happy without knowing who you're changing things *with*."

A burst of laughter from the huge tent broke through the splashing fountains, and Suzanne didn't need to be there to see it.

Chanelle with one perfectly pink-manicured hand to her throat, head tilted back just enough to show off how smooth and tight the skin under her throat still was at age say-she-doesn't-look-a-day-over-forty-but-we-all-know-she's-really-sixty-three.

She claimed the glories of her McGill-Candler ancestry accounted for the miraculous resistance to aging.

To her credit—and her surgeon's—the scars truly were hard to spot.

And everyone gathered around her would fawn and fuss and make much of her.

Like everyone always had.

Every single day of her life.

No matter how much good she could do with all the lucky breaks life had handed her.

Or what kind of moldy skeletons waited to caper out of her family money's closet.

"I don't know how much *happy* factors into it anymore." Suzanne knew her smile wouldn't fool anyone at all, much less the one who'd taught her how to fake a good one in the first place. "And I get the feeling I might regret this before long, so maybe take a minute or two to think it over before you tell me anything. But I'm still glad to see you, Leslie. And I'm listening."

Leslie raised her eyebrows and sighed.

"I thought about it plenty before I drove down here, trust me. And on the drive, and all night last night, and this morning. The whole time I hung back and watched you during this vapid little ceremony, and right up until I touched your shoulder. I hope this isn't the last time we see each other, and that's the truth. I've missed you like crazy. But I know it's a real possibility."

"Yet here we are."

"Here we are. Okay. Ms. McGill-Candler over there came by her money the old-fashioned way. By popping into the world in the right place at the right time to the right people. The family fortunes are a little shady, like most that were piled up before this dear old nation of ours started paying attention to such things. And since they quit paying attention again. Things changed when Chanelle herself took the reins."

Suzanne's gaze wandered back toward that damn basement again, zeroing in on the likely weak spot of the sliding glass doors. Sure, times had changed since she and Leslie got into this game back in the 1980s, before security systems and miniature cameras and computers in everyone's pockets took a hell of a lot of fun out of it.

And added an unacceptable level of risk as it turned out.

However, she knew too much about the overconfidence of human nature—especially when it came to certain types of humans—to think someone was watching all the things all the time.

And too much about Leslie to suspect this would turn out to be an impossible gig.

Unless that meant impossible to turn down.

"All right then, what changed with Chanelle?"

Leslie raised one eyebrow and glanced toward the house herself.

"She got a little too drunk on her own power, you might say. Decided serving on a dozen different boards of directors and organizing flashy charity events and throwing the best parties since the Clinton Administration simply weren't enough excitement for her blood. So she started taking advantage of her special access."

"She's not stealing money," Suzanne said. "That doesn't fit the pattern for someone like this. Too easily uncovered."

"You're right." Leslie winked and pulled out a smartphone that should have been too big to hide in her pretty skirt's pocket. "All her financials check out, all the way down to accurately reporting all those sweet charitable donations and huge piles of legitimate deductions. She's not even taking a salary from any of her many obligations and generous gifts of her time."

She pulled up a vivid photo on the huge screen, showing two men in a rather intimate position. Followed by two women, and a man and two women. Then a series of couples of all varieties, all similarly exposed and otherwise occupied.

"Wait," Suzanne said, touching Leslie's arm. "I recognize some of them."

"You'd recognize even more if we wandered over there to the big fancy tent party. See, Chanelle's game isn't embezzling or tax fraud or sneaking precious artwork out of museums. She's into blackmail, especially of the sexual variety. Her favorites are closeted gay or lesbian or bi folks, but she dabbles in secret polyamorous relationships or catching people cheating. Anything that can gain her that much more leverage and power over your little group down here."

Suzanne's skin rippled with queasy gooseflesh, and her belly turned cold.

"That kind of thing can get people *killed* down here, and a lot of other places too, sick as it makes me to say so. We're not exactly in an era of growing acceptance in certain parts of the country. Turns out a whole lot of unstable people weren't too thrilled with changing the definition of marriage."

Leslie closed her eyes for a second, and when she opened them her face was filled with regret.

"I know this is going to come across as a low blow, especially with your situation. I truly am sorry about that. But you're the only person I could dig up who might be able to help put a stop to this before she gets even worse. Before someone else gets hurt."

Now Suzanne regretted finishing her coffee, because her whole gut felt full of hot churning acid. She clutched her empty mug until her fingers ached.

Only one other person on Earth had known everything she'd gotten into over the years besides the woman in front of her. And Dawn had loved her anyway, and brought her down to Atlanta and shown her a different way to do good things.

A way that still involved elaborate plans and illusions, but not nearly so much breaking and entering or theft or risk of going to prison.

Dawn had introduced Suzanne to Ms. Chanelle McGill-Candler and almost everyone else still laughing and chatting under the party tent, mainly because Dawn and Chanelle had known each other since they were girls.

Much like Suzanne and Leslie had.

Chanelle had gone to great pains to express sympathy when Dawn got sick, and she'd shown up at the funeral full of flowers and hugs and promises to keep Suzanne involved.

And she had.

All while risking the health, happiness, and possibly the lives of other couples she claimed to be friends with.

"Did she have...Were there...Does Chanelle have photos of me and Dawn in her sick little collection of blackmail bait?"

Leslie shook her head and squeezed Suzanne's hand for a second.

"Not that I've ever seen or heard of. We think we've got access to all of her files, and none of the date-stamps go that far back. She seems to have gotten started with her nasty hobby after…I really am sorry about how that went down, Suz."

Suzanne nodded and blinked through tears that were more anger than sorrow in that moment.

"What do you need me to do?"

She was grateful Leslie didn't bother pretending or hesitating now that the information was out in the open.

"Right now, the house's security system is set on minimum. All the better to play a good hostess in case someone needs the restroom. And as far as we can tell, the secret vault isn't far from the basement restroom. No one has gotten close enough to tell for sure, but from the blueprints plus data patterns and power usage, it's in a closet to the left of those doors."

"And you want me to go in there and grab what? A laptop? A hard drive?"

Leslie changed the image on her phone's screen to show a silver and gray device that didn't look any bigger than a deck of playing cards.

"She probably has several copies after all the money and trouble she spent to gather evidence. But from the address and serial number skimmed out of her network, she has more than enough stored on this little solid-state drive. I'd say she uses it for daily backups. It will be enough, and a lot easier to get than a laptop. I can get you a five-minute window with no security cameras or the closet door lock engaged, but I can't promise longer."

The sickening fury in Suzanne's chest gave way enough to let a sliver of excitement slip through. The first time she'd let herself get fired up over a gig for a long, long time.

But her need to plan and study and understand all the risks involved—and the rewards—didn't entirely go away simply because she'd been out of the game for so long.

"Who are you working with, Les?" Suzanne felt bad, saying those words. But that didn't change the fact that she needed to say them. "Did you switch sides? Should I be watching what I say because you're not the only one listening in?"

Leslie shook her head without looking away from Suzanne's eyes.

"Not yet, and hopefully not ever. I've learned a lot since we quit working together, but I never forgot what you taught me about keeping myself safe. I've got other partners now, yeah. And none of us can manage to get inside and back out again."

"And these partners trust me even though they don't know me?"

"They trust you because they know *me*. I told

them we wouldn't find a better way into that house without years of work. And that even if you turned me down, you wouldn't turn me in. Was I wrong?"

Suzanne examined the house and the yard and the sliding glass doors again, with a far more professional and serious eye.

If the closet really was that close, and security truly was that low, the gig should be a walk in the backyard that looked an awful lot like a park.

If the things Leslie said and showed her were true, this was a job well worth doing.

But the risk...

"I know this isn't what you want to hear," Suzanne said, "but I haven't seen or talked to you for more than ten years. I don't know whoever you're working with at all. As it stands right now, I'm taking on a hell of a lot of the burden without much to back it up. I *know* what a good actor you are, Leslie. You taught me everything *I* know. I'd be crazy to do this with almost nothing to go on."

"But you want to anyway. I can see it in your eyes, same as when we were fourteen years old and had no idea what we were getting into. You can't tell me the idea hasn't got you, all along your chest and belly and spine. All the way into that big brain of yours that made everything work out as well as it did for us all those years."

Suzanne stared up at the cloudless blue sky, resisting the urge to check out the basement doors yet again.

Every word was real and true, and way too accurate for her to argue with.

None of that meant she had to return to the same path she'd stumbled onto long before she possibly could have known better.

"Everything worked out until it didn't, Les. That's why I got out, and you know it. I'll cover you if you want to go inside and make a run at it. Or I'll meet these people you're working with and see what they're all about. If what you're telling me about Chanelle is true, then she absolutely needs to go down, and hard. But today's not the day for the job. Not if you want me to do it."

Leslie didn't say anything for a long time, and Suzanne wasn't sure she was still breathing. All around them, the cool April breeze played with the fountains, and the babble of voices from the canape tent carried on.

Inside, those poor confused kids probably avoided looking at each other for fear of laughing out loud and having to try to explain what was so funny, while one of them wondered what the heck they were going to do with a silver spade.

Somewhere in the sand-colored sprawl of the

McGill-Candler estate house, a collection of obscene and vicious photos and possibly videos waited to blow up people's lives. Some of them innocent, some of them not so much.

Some of them under that ostentatious tent right that minute.

None of them with any clue how much hell was headed their way.

Suzanne had that clue, and she knew it had to be stopped.

Every bit as much as she knew it would all blow up in her face if she walked in there without understanding exactly what she was getting into.

She hoped her old friend and partner in crime would understand that, too.

Leslie slowly shook her head, but with the faint trace of a smile.

"Want to know the part I left out?" she said. "Not about the house, or what Chanelle's doing, or how much we have figured out already. I told my partners there was no *way* you'd go for it today. Not without getting every scrap of information you could first. I told them you'd figure out a better way to go about it if we'd let you. Was I wrong?"

Suzanne shook her head in return.

And a smile found its way to her lips whether she wanted it to or not.

"I'm sure you're wrong about all kinds of things, Les. I guess we'll get a chance to figure them all out, once we get done with everything I've messed up since we last talked."

She waved her arm toward the estate's parking lot, tastefully hidden behind the sound-blocking row of hedges. Because the sight of even expensive, well-maintained vehicles simply would not do in such a setting.

"No, you weren't wrong. Some habits never die. They just hide out until it's safe to get started again. Let's get out of here and decide what we're going to do about it."

THE TELLTALE SCRAPE

DAVID H. HENDRICKSON

If I hadn't been paying attention, I'd have become just another sucker. The whole lot of us would have gotten cleaned out. Sucked dry. No different than all the others in this place.

The jangling and clanging of slot machines echoed from adjoining rooms where fools did the equivalent of inserting a dollar and getting back seventy-five or at best eight-five cents. They believed in Lady Luck, urging her on either silently or prayerfully or vocally at full volume. Then, hours later, they'd wonder where all their money had gone and why Lady Luck had betrayed them.

Slightly less foolish, but still fools, were those of all ages and descriptions who surrounded the roulette wheel or craps tables or the carnival games —Mississippi stud, Three-card poker, and Crazy Fours for starters—and bellowed even louder to Lady Luck over the music blaring from the loudspeakers. They laughed and cheered when she temporarily heard their prayers, bestowing upon them her bounty of large mounds of chips, but then groaned and even cried out in pain when she betrayed them, taking away all that she had given them and more. Almost always, much, much more.

And if Lady Luck did not betray them on this evening, she would work harder next time and eventually would betray them all.

I never understood those fools. I got no rush from flushing my money down the casino toilet. Its allure mystified me. I could only respect those who played blackjack and Spanish 21 with strategic prowess and especially the select members of their clan with a gift for counting cards. They were the only ones who had a shot at beating the house.

My only slightly above average memory fell far short of the threshold for counting cards—and not just because of taking too many blows to the head as a collegiate linebacker—so I viewed the suckers elsewhere in the casino from my intellectually superior vantage of a seat at the poker table. The casino took its cut of a few chips out of every pot, but I was pitting my skills not against an unbeatable house but against the seven other players at my table. And some of them were as mathematically moronic as their nitwit brethren throughout the casino willingly lining up to face the casino's financial firing squad, its slot machines and table games mowing down their victims without mercy.

Today was the grand opening of yet another casino in southern New Hampshire, close enough to the Massachusetts border to entice Massholes like me to cross over the state line, but still subject to the New Hampshire gaming laws. And not just any new casino. I'd played poker many times with its silver-haired, sunglasses-wearing, cowboy-hatted owner, Dick Hannigan, and when I'd seen him in previous weeks, he'd always invited me to the grand opening.

"You'll never come back to this pigsty again," he said each time, gesturing to whatever poker room we happened to be playing in.

The comment garnered dirty looks from whomever the dealer was at that particular table. Hannigan had even gotten a tap on the shoulder once or twice and a request to leave the premises, but you had to give him credit for trying.

And I was certain to take him up on the offer. Not because I had anything against pigsties. When I'm not making half my living at the poker table, I'm a private eye whose office is a seedy bar called Original Sin with its most conspicuous other residents being hookers, a drug dealer, and of course the usual alcoholics and other lowlifes.

Pigsties are my life.

If there's money to be made in a pigsty, you'll see my six-two, two-hundred-twenty-pound muscular frame wading happily into the muck, the only thing clean being my freshly shaved scalp. But I'll also play poker wherever I can make the most money. Amateurs care about ambience and amenities, but as a pro I'll go wherever the suckers go.

And suckers tend to be drawn to Grand Openings. So I was here to separate those suckers from their money.

The Granite State Simply Spectacular Casino was no pigsty. Every slot machine glistened. Chrome countertops, railings, and edgings sparkled. All ten of the eight-player poker tables in this enclosed room featured impeccably new green felt. Hi-Def, flat-screen TVs spaced twenty feet apart and tuned primarily to sports contests adorned the walls. Attractive waitresses and waiters, smelling sweetly of perfume or cologne, moved from table to table, taking and delivering drink orders above the din of conversation, laughter, and groans of frustration. All the tables were full or nearly so with patrons from the lowest-stakes game to my table, one of two high-stakes No-Limit Hold 'Em tables.

Arguably, the only flaw I could see in the entire place was that like most smaller casinos but unlike the largest ones, there were no automatic shuffling machines, forcing the dealers to shuffle the cards manually. That did reduce the number of hands dealt each hour, and therefore cut into my hourly rate of profit, but I could live with that wherever the game was good.

And holy smokes, the game was good. One of

the other seven seats at the table was empty, but otherwise there was an unusually weak collection of players, most of them either timid or foolishly reckless, thinking they were playing on TV, or so easy to read for someone like me they might as well be playing with their cards turned face up.

The kind of crowd drawn to a Grand Opening like moths to a flame.

And baby, I was the flame. Dressed in my jeans and T-shirt, Red Sox cap, and sunglasses, I'd grown my original chip stack of a thousand dollars—the maximum allowed in New Hampshire—to fifteen hundred in less than an hour. I was seated to the left of the dealer in seat six, and the two weakest players were to my right in seats seven and eight, up against the dealer, an ideal position for me to make large raises after they bet and isolate them.

The table was a license to print money. I sipped at my Coke—only an idiot on par with the slot-machine fools drinks alcohol at the table—put the plastic cup back in the holder, and prepared to print myself some more Benjamins.

The weak player in seat seven next to me, a sixty-year-old thin, bald gentleman in a charcoal gray suit and tie was pulling in a pot of over a thousand dollars when a pro I recognized named Ralphie Sanders sat down in the empty seat directly opposite me.

Good news, bad news.

Good news that the weak player next to me had just scored a huge windfall in classic headshaking fashion, chasing a twelve-to-one long shot to the final card and hitting it despite his opponent's previous bets making it a mathematically losing strategy to keep chasing. His suddenly red-faced opponent was cursing the player as well as his own Lady Luck, but it's always good news when the worst players get more chips to eventually give to you.

The bad news, of course, was the arrival of another pro, effectively slicing into my expected profits. I turned around and surveyed the other high-stakes table and recognized no one. No pros. Perhaps no one as weak as the two players to my right, but the presence of another pro here was a huge variable in the profitability equation.

"Don't bother," Ralphie Sanders, my fellow professional, said. "I've already requested a table change."

I nodded, grinning. "Great minds think alike."

"Devious ones, too," he said, and we went back, like circling sharks, to observing the fish who would be our next meal.

THE TELLTALE SCRAPE

Ralphie's switch to the other high-stakes table coincided with a new player arriving to replace him, a short, squat guy going for the tough-guy, gangster look. Mid-twenties with jet black hair slicked back. Designer sunglasses, a Rolex knockoff on one thick wrist, and a gold bracelet on the other. Diamond-studded pinkie rings. He unracked his mix of black and red chips totaling the thousand-dollar maximum and stacked them in front of his seat against the rail, then ordered a Jack and Coke from the waitress. Until I heard otherwise, I decided his name would be Gangster Boy.

A few hands later, we got a new dealer, a pretty young woman with flowing black hair down to her slender shoulders, a model's complexion, and exceptionally long fake eyelashes. She tapped out our existing dealer, an older, stocky, balding guy named Otto, who moved on to the other high-stakes table. Her nameplate read Nona. The thing that was instantly memorable about her, other than her undeniable beauty, were her long fingernails painted with celebratory tiny white explosions against a background of alternating red and blue—red on the thumb, middle, and pinkie fingers, blue on the index and ring fingers.

"Gorgeous!" said a leering middle-aged man with salt-and-pepper hair seated to the right of Gangster Boy, then added, "And the fingernails, too!" He chuckled at his own joke, joined by a few others, and gave Nona a wink.

Nona responded with a frozen smile and shuffled the cards.

My hackles rose. I'd seen this movie a few too many times. The attractive young woman would invariably get tipped by the male patrons better than her counterparts, but she'd all too often pay for it by having to fend off continued unwanted flirtation and even increasingly suggestive remarks. I kept my eyes on the jerk, prepared to say something if necessary.

Nothing unusual happened for several hands, other than the middle-aged flirt offering up to Nona his name and occupation—"I'm Charlie, a lawyer, a *very successful* lawyer"—as if that would simply melt the panties off of her. But again, she just flashed her frozen smile, panties apparently intact.

I silently established the odds that Charlie was in fact his real name as a near-prohibitive favorite, perhaps three grand to win a hundred, but that he was no more a lawyer, much less a very successful one, than I was. I make my living both at the poker table and as a private eye by being able to read people, and for me, Charlie was an open book. As a result, I established the mythical wagering line on his occupation being true as a seven-to-one dog, figuring I could get mythical action on that number even though my true read gave it as closer to thirty-to-one.

The things I do to keep myself amused and mentally alert.

A few hands later, the sound of Nona's dealing changed ever so slightly. It was subtle, but I detected a slight scraping sound as she dealt several cards.

No question about it. Scraping.

No one else at the table appeared to notice.

And then it was gone.

The fingernails, I figured. Had to be the long fingernails. As she dealt a card, it must be making that sound as it slid past one of those beautiful, long, painted nails with the tiny white explosions against an alternating backdrop of red and blue.

Had to be.

But why had I heard that scraping sound for several cards and then not at all?

I looked at Nona to get a read, but could detect nothing definitive. Even so, I felt a sense of unease. My instincts told me something was wrong. Or at least possibly so. I wouldn't bet the ranch on it, but my suspicions were raised.

"Your bet," she said, pointing to Charlie, the allegedly very successful lawyer.

Charlie appeared to be searching for some double entendre to respond with, but coming up dry, just smiled and limped in with the minimum bet. Two more limpers followed suit.

I held a hand just barely good enough to play in my position. A classic raise or fold decision. And if I raised, it would have to be a big one. I'd happily do that to isolate against the two weak players to my right, but Charlie presented a problem. He could be slow playing a huge hand, hopeful to show off his trapping prowess for Nona, or he could also have a marginal hand but would refuse to be bullied off it and appear weak to Nona. That looked like a fifty-fifty proposition. Then there were the four players still to act after me including Gangster Boy, about whom I had not yet gained any useful objective information.

And there was also that disquieting scraping sound.

I tossed my hand away, then applied a laser focus on all the cards in play. Was Nona inadvertently marking the cards with her amazing nails? If so, I needed to see it immediately, or at least before anyone else did, and ask for a deck change.

Or could she somehow be marking the cards intentionally?

No, couldn't be. Almost always, any marking was done by players while the card, almost always an ace or king, was in their hand, after which they could see it in other players' hands in subsequent rounds.

No way Nona was intentionally marking cards. I was sure of it, even after reminding myself not to assume her innocence simply because she was gorgeous. How many men over the decades had fallen victim to that trap? Not me, at least not now. If she was marking the cards, it was accidental and a problem easily solved by nail clippers, no matter how agonizing to clip off those works of art.

I'd seen no markings on my cards before I discarded them and could detect none on anyone else's. Coincidentally, though, Gangster Boy won a big pot holding pocket aces in his hand.

Hmmm. I'm not one to believe in coincidences, so I shifted my suspicions out of low gear.

But for the next eight hands, there was nothing to see or hear. No marked cards. No scraping. Mick Flanagan, the paranoid fool, strikes again. Making something out of nothing.

Until the scraping began again as Nona dealt.

What the...

It struck me like a heavyweight's left hook coming out of nowhere. A slobberknocker that left me flat on the canvas seeing stars.

Nona was a cheat.

She was a card mechanic. She was setting the deck as she shuffled, then with the plastic cut card on the bottom to prevent dealing off the bottom, she was "deuce dealing," dealing not the top card but the second from the top. Having set an ace or a king on the top, she saved it by dealing the second card until she got to the other half of the team.

Gangster Boy.

At least that was my theory. I'd never seen it happen in person, only heard about it, and even then only in crooked home games. I couldn't be sure it was happening here until I actually saw the telltale signs. I'd only heard the subtle scraping sound, a telltale sound to be sure, but one that could be defended as an innocent byproduct of Nona's beautiful nails. I had to see her slide the top two cards ever so slightly off the top of the deck with the thumb holding the deck, and then use the forefinger of the other hand to slide the second card out, the act that causes the scraping sound.

Had to see it with my own eyes.

In fact, detecting that miniscule sliding of the two cards would be nearly impossible. The key would be watching Nona's thumb. Normally, dealers lift their left thumb off the deck with every card dealt. But when deuce dealing, the thumb moves side to side.

It was too late now, but I'd need to see all of that in a future hand to know for sure. I'd also need to somehow pay such extreme attention to her hand movements without tipping off her or Gangster Boy to my suspicions.

Good luck with that.

From behind my sunglasses, I looked at Nona and then Gangster Boy. Nona betrayed nothing and Gangster Boy was such a caricature of macho posturing it was hard to separate the obvious BS from a possible tell.

I looked down at my hand, prepared to throw it out regardless of the two cards. Only a fool plays against a team in a rigged game.

Ace of clubs. Queen of hearts.

I had all I could do to keep from betraying my inner dismay. Had to maintain my poker face, my steady hands, and my even breathing.

An amateur would have groaned. Closed his eyes in frustration. Or decided that he wasn't really all that sure the game was rigged after all. He couldn't possibly discard a hand like ace-queen.

I am not an amateur.

In a clean game, I'd play this hand in my current position every day unless I was facing a gigantic raise, especially from a strong opponent. I wouldn't get carried away with the hand. Ace-queen was too easily dominated by ace-king, aces, kings, or queens. But it would take a lot to force me to lay the hand down.

A rigged game amounts to a lot.

I wanted nothing to do with this hand, but I'd have to be careful my cards didn't flip over when I discarded them. Folding ace-queen would set off all kinds of alarm bells, practically announcing to the cheaters that I was onto them.

The question was whether Nona had set the deck thoroughly or just enough to feed the one card, the ace or king on the top, to Gangster Boy. Sometimes his second card would be unplayable junk, but starting with a first card ace or king provided a dominating advantage. I was going to gamble on the latter, that she'd been able to only manipulate that one card and had no idea what was in my hand. I didn't see how she could do more. If I was wrong, I'd bet all the chips in the casino I'd be able to see some reaction from the two.

THE TELLTALE SCRAPE

I tossed my cards low and into the muck, careful not to risk them flipping over or even showing a mere hint as to their value, and watched Nona and Gangster Boy from behind my sunglasses.

Nothing.

Which meant Nona was only cheating while dealing the second card and nothing more. She didn't know what I had tossed out. No one could have known I'd made such a discard and not shown any reaction at all.

So I waited for the hand to play out and shock of all shocks, Gangster Boy won again. He didn't have to show his cards because everyone folded to his large bet, but he either held a monster hand or was a brilliant player able to push the rest of the table around with impunity.

Five hands later, I saw all I needed to see. The telltale scraping sound and the telltale movement of Nona's thumb. Gangster Boy winning another big pot.

Technically, I could have brought in the floor manager, a portly, middle-aged guy in a black suit and tie with a florid complexion. It was his job to enforce rules, handle disputes, and oversee the room. Unfortunately, I'd seen him in action—or more accurately, *inaction*—at other poker rooms and he always chose the path of least resistance. Did the absolute least required to do his job.

The ultimate empty suit.

Even if I got him to surreptitiously observe the table—and he'd be about as surreptitious as a three-hundred pound wild gorilla—his response to even the most blatant cheating would be to warn the offenders to knock it off. He'd probably even offer a friendly smile while he did it.

I had to go over his head direct to Dick Hannigan, the owner.

Hannigan wasn't hard to find. Silver-haired, middle-aged men wearing large gray cowboy hats might be prevalent in Texas, but not here in New Hampshire. His Stetson might as well have been a flashing green neon sign. He was striding along the middle of seven aisles of clanging slot machines, glancing to both sides with approval. He always wore sunglasses while at the poker table as did I, but had dispensed with them today. Apparently he'd figured his bright blue eyes were better off seen as he gladhanded his way through the crowds, shaking hands and patting shoulders as long as that didn't distract the suckers from filling his coffers with their hard-earned cash.

Those eyes brightened when he saw me coming. He flashed a used-car salesman's bright smile and extended his hand.

"Mick, great to see you!"

I took his hand, steered him away from the nearest patrons for privacy, and while watching his every reaction whispered, "You have a problem. One of your high-stakes poker tables is crooked."

He rocked back on his heels as if I'd struck him. He blinked several times. "Why do you say that?"

"A dealer is working with one of the players. Deuce dealing to feed him cards. I can show you on the cameras."

"That's impossible! I don't believe you!"

"Let me show you. You do have cameras going don't you?"

"Of course," he said, but with the red-faced bluster of a philandering husband caught in the act. He was lying his ass off. I could read him like a book. The cameras were not running, at least not on the poker room.

Perhaps deliberately so.

"Then let me show you," I said, knowing his answer.

Hannigan swallowed hard and looked away. "I can't allow that."

"Why?"

"You're a customer. Customers are never allowed to see the cameras."

If I suspected he was lying before, I was sure of it now. Customers were indeed routinely forbidden access to the cameras that recorded games to insure against cheating. But there was a hint of fear in his voice and the mannerisms of a poker player bluffing with a losing hand.

"I'm not just any customer, Dick," I said firmly. "You know me. I'm trying to protect you. Let you deal with it quietly before it takes down your entire casino."

"Don't threaten me! Don't you dare threaten me!"

"I'm not threatening you. I came directly to you to protect you. But you have to deal with it. I won't let you turn a blind eye while the other players at that table are getting ripped off."

"No one else knows?" he asked with a quick glance around.

And with those words and actions, I knew.

Dick Hannigan was in on the whole scam. Had either set it up and was taking his cut as the third member of the team, or was allowing it to happen, perhaps as a favor owed to the wrong person or to pay off a debt.

It wasn't enough that he was taking all the other suckers in the casino to the cleaners. The little old ladies flushing their life savings down the slot machine toilet. The men and women of all ages plowing through their payroll checks at the craps tables and roulette wheels before the weekend was even half over, sure they could defy the mathematics that would inevitably ground them to a pulp.

That wasn't enough for a guy like Dick Hannigan.

He had to take those of us at the poker table, convinced we were merely matching wits and strategic decisions with each other, and by rigging the game, turn us into suckers, too.

When I got back to the table, Gangster Boy and Nona were nowhere to be found, not at my table or anywhere else in the poker room. My chips had already been racked into plastic trays. Two tall, beefy members of security clad in black uniforms and caps, one white and the other African American, stood behind the wide-eyed floor manager who looked like he was about to pee his pants.

He swallowed hard. "You've got to leave, Mick, and you're never to return. It's a lifetime ban."

"Based on what?" I asked. I pointed to the others at the table. "Based on trying to protect these players from a rigged game?"

The players stared at me with deer-in-the-headlights looks.

"The lifetime ban is for you cheating," the terrified floor manager said, his voice quivering and his eyes unable to meet mine.

"Me cheating?" I said, then turned to the other players. "The cute dealer with the fingernails was feeding aces to Gangster Boy, who I'm sure has already cashed out his chips and left. You didn't realize it, but you know I'm right. They were stealing your money."

"I want my money back!" demanded Charlie the alleged lawyer, his lust for Nona suddenly gone.

The white security guard stepped between me and the table.

"Sir, leave now and you'll be allowed to cash out your chips," he said. "Another word and we'll carry you out, perhaps on a stretcher, and you can go to court to get your money back."

I shook my head in disgust, then shouldered

past the security guard and picked up the two trays filled with my chips. Before I turned to leave, I fixed the other players with my eyes. I didn't need to say anything more. They'd been warned. If they continued to play here, they were even bigger fools than all the ones I turned my nose up at the slot machines.

Lambs to the slaughter.

As for me, if this was a mobbed-up casino in the old days, I'd be certain to disappear the moment I stepped outside and be buried in an unmarked grave. Fortunately, this wasn't the old days and this casino wasn't mobbed up. No one was going to make me disappear.

Unfortunately for Dick Hannigan, I wasn't going to disappear at all. I was going straight to the gaming commission, the local papers, and maybe even the *Boston Globe*. And of course to that font of truth, honesty, and protecting the little guy—the Internet.

Hannigan would almost certainly get away with it. Deny, deny, deny. Without video recordings, the evidence was too scant to prove guilt. Nona and Gangster Boy would lay low until the fools and the suckers chose to forget what they hadn't wanted to hear in the first place.

You can't always protect lambs from the slaughter. You just have to do the best you can.

A CLASSIC CASE OF MISDIRECTION

JOHANNA ROTHMAN

Closing the door behind her with a quiet snick, the dual odors of stale coffee and pizza gave Jayne Stone that roller coaster feeling in her stomach. Clearly, at least one of the team had been here, in GenResearch Security Central, for hours.

Based in a nondescript four-story brick building in a nondescript office park in bucolic Waltham, Massachusetts, the Security team had a small room protected from outsiders in the very middle of the fourth floor, sandwiched between the elevators and the stairs.

With no windows, the room was large enough for four sixty-inch monitors across the top of the room, one monitor for each time zone. Below the monitors were floor-to-ceiling whiteboards. Right now, the left-most whiteboard had the word "URGENT!" in big red letters and several yellow stickies underneath. The right-most whiteboard had several black sketches under the title of "Possibilities." The two middle whiteboards had the faint outlines of previous sketches and notes.

Directly in front of her were four white workstations—really, just adjustable desks, each with two large monitors and ergonomic black chairs. When Jayne had designed the room, she'd created enough room for all four people on her team to roll over to each other or to work alone. Now, there was just one person to her far right, Elmer Jones, his fingers punching the keys. He had his deep blue headphones on, which meant he was concentrating. She could tell how upset Elmer was by the volume of his keystrokes. He was pretty upset because she could barely hear the air filtration over his keyboard pounding.

The pizza box was next to him—half of a pepperoni and mushroom pizza still uneaten. Maybe the pizza wasn't that old, because it still smelled great.

When she'd had a chance to choose where to locate the Security team, she'd chosen a place where the team could fly under the radar. As a result, only the Sales team was in Cambridge, two blocks down from MIT. Everyone else was out here in the suburbs, flying under the radar. Jayne had discovered early on that it was useful to fly under the radar, in effect to have a little misdirection. For the product, the research, and her career.

A little misdirection went a long way. For all of the security risks, software and physical.

But right now, she needed direction, so she scanned the monitors, looking for red dots that would show all the compromised locations. The attack was clearly underway, with red dots filling the Eastern-most monitor, and slowly proceeding west. It almost looked like the attack the team had stopped, just two weeks ago.

The attack was much worse in Cambridge, where the big Sales meeting was supposed to take place at ten this morning.

She glanced at her watch—just six in the morning. She'd been running downstairs at the gym when her watch had beeped to notify her of a security breach. She'd managed to take a shower and dress at top speed. Now, fifteen minutes later, she glanced down—yes, her shirt was fully buttoned and her dress jeans were zipped up. She'd even remembered to drag on a gray cardigan, because the people here loved to keep this room ice-cube cold. Even in late June. Maybe especially in late June, just before July fourth.

Jayne involuntarily shivered. This was going to be really bad. She corrected herself—it was already was.

Now that she'd oriented herself, she looked at Elmer. He was still nodding his head and stabbing his keyboard. She waved in his direction to get his attention.

He took off his headset and shook his head. "Boss, this is bad. Really bad." He reached for a piece of pizza. Then he pointed and asked, "You want?"

She shook her head and said, "No, thanks. I'll get a more conventional breakfast later."

He shrugged. "Well. It's got all the food groups. And it's still warm."

She shook her head again and asked, "What do you know aside from what's on the monitors?" she asked.

"It's an inside job."

Her breath stuttered. She dragged over a chair and half-crumpled, half-sat down. "You're sure?"

"I am. They didn't even do a good job of covering their tracks. Look over here."

He pointed his greasy finger on the monitor.

It was a good thing it wasn't her monitor. She hated fingerprints on her monitors.

"See this? It's the open door. They even left their password for me to find. 'OpenSesame'."

"Why would they leave tracks like that? Are you sure it's not some form of misdirection?"

Elmer took another bite, and frowned. "Nope. This is where they entered," he pointed. "Then, they bounced around, changed a few passwords, changed a few settings—which I put back—and now they're like a shark, lying in wait."

She looked at him. Then, she looked back at the screen. "You really have a way with words."

"That's not the worst part," he said. "The worst

part is it came from inside this building. From 'Executive Row' where all the managers sit."

She felt her stomach tighten—the roller coaster was not yet over. "Our senior management? One of our managers?"

He took a big bite and said, "Yup." He paused to chew. "In fact, it came from your office."

That's when the lights went out.

Along with the lights, all the ambient noise died.

Jayne had to remember to breathe. And to count to five.

Jayne thought the odors of coffee and pizza seemed more intense without any lights. Worse, her head started to pound with the idea that someone had framed her for this breach. But she said, "We should have everything back by the count of five."

Elmer started to count and by the time he got to four, all the lights came back on. "That was pretty scary," he said.

"Yeah, this room has a separate generator for electricity and air. But it takes a little bit for it to kick in. There's also another egress—"

"Egress?" he said. "Not exit? No backdoor?"

She sighed. "Fine. Exit. I had the contractors put another exit in, because there's no window and it's not safe to have just one door."

Elmer turned and looked at her. "And let me guess. There's no evidence of that on the building specs."

"Well, the fire department has the right specs," she said and grinned. "But here? Our management? No."

"You didn't trust them when we moved here?"

"I'm in security. I don't trust anyone."

Elmer offered a short laugh. "Well, we are the suspicious people." He stopped laughing and finished chewing. "So who wants to frame you for this? Who would do this?"

Jayne thought. Then she said, "Well, I'm the newest senior manager here. And I'm just a director, not a VP. When I explained we needed different controls for what we downloaded and what we shared, everyone was angry. But the two angriest people were Chris Berman, our CEO, and Rachel Cox, the VP of Sales. One of the investor groups insisted they hire me."

Elmer smiled. "They had no idea how much of a hard-ass you are."

Jayne raised an eyebrow.

"Not as a manager," he said. "As a security geek."

"When I got here," she said, "I was surprised things were working as well as they were. Because I was pretty sure they shared secrets with a different investor group on that last round of funding."

Elmer whistled, long and slow. "Is that illegal?"

Jayne shook her head. "At the least, it's shady. Unethical. But Illegal? I couldn't find direct evidence. So I left it and instituted new procedures."

Elmer smiled. "The hard-ass stuff."

She nodded.

That's when the red dots began to creep across the monitors, from right to left.

"Holy—" Elmer said. "I gotta get to this."

"You do that. I need to go to my office and see what's going on. At the very least, change my password. Do me a favor, please."

Elmer looked at her. "Of course."

"Let's leave a chat open, so I can let you know when I see something."

Elmer wiped his hands with a napkin and pulled out his phone. "Open now."

"Thanks," she said.

He pulled his blue headphones back on before he continued to stab at the keyboard.

Jayne left, closing the door behind her. She had a date with her office and computer.

Five minutes later, Jayne stood at her office door. She hadn't seen anyone in the halls, but it was only six thirty in the morning. People normally strolled in closer to nine. And today, they might be at the big Sales meeting in Cambridge.

Her corporate-gray-painted office looked the same, from her adjustable fake-wood desk on the left with the locking matching credenza behind it, to her matching round visitor table with its two black chairs on the right.

She had a black ergonomic chair which was more comfortable than the visitor chairs, but they were adequate.

Behind the visitor table was her "visitor" whiteboard, where she and her team could collaborate with sketches. Her personal whiteboard was on the wall to the left of the office door. Those had To Do and Not To Do columns, with notes and yellow stickies.

She was thankful that she had a large window that overlooked the parking lot. Not that the parking lot was so great, but she appreciated seeing

—and sometimes walking—the curved walking paths.

But something smelled off. As if someone had dumped aftershave on the rug.

She looked down. The dark gray low-nap rug—just a few shades darker than the paint—looked clean.

What did she expect to see? A sign that said, "I was here and framed you for a security breach."

Clearly not.

She sat down behind her desk, where the odor was much stronger. She didn't know what the odor was, but she would be able to identify the person wearing it.

Elmer texted her: "The attacks multiplied. Do something."

That rollercoaster feeling was back. She was not staying under the radar and was clearly not applying any misdirection.

She sat down and tried to log in.

She saw the message, "Incorrect password."

Maybe she'd made a mistake?

She retyped her login. And saw the same message.

She decided to change her password. She tried. But all she saw was, "Incorrect password. You are now locked out."

She converted her text with Elmer to a call. She said, "I'm locked out and can't change my password."

"So am I."

Jayne got cold at the thought that neither of them was able to change their passwords, leaving their data in the hands of the people who breached the system.

"I'll be right over."

She stood and stuck her phone in her jeans pocket, all set to leave. That's when both Chris Berman and Rachel Cox appeared in her doorway. He was in a gray pinstripe suit. She was in a bright red form-fitting dress.

Jayne always thought they were attractive people. Chris, with his blonde hair and blue eyes. Rachel with her dark, curly, long hair and green eyes. But Jayne had clearly missed the fact that they were a couple.

A solid misdirection on their part.

The strong odor emanated from one of them. Jayne suspected it was Chris' aftershave.

"Excuse me," she said. "I need to get to Security Central."

Rachel walked into the room, tossing her long dark hair over one shoulder. "I don't think you need to go anywhere," she said. "You need to stay right here."

Jayne hoped that Elmer heard that.

Jayne continued to stand behind her desk. "What do you want?"

Rachel laughed.

Jayne thought it was an ugly laugh, full of scorn and contempt.

"I want the keys to the kingdom," she said. "Hand over the master password."

Jayne shook her head. "It doesn't work that way. There is no single master password. So you can't have it."

"Then I'll take yours."

Jayne shrugged. "You can have it, but it no longer works. And I can't change it. Which one of you changed it?"

Rachel's face got red. "How dare you imply that one of us changed your password?"

"Someone did," Jayne said. "And if it wasn't you, it was probably him."

She gestured to Chris, who now stood just behind Rachel, but off to her left.

Rachel swirled, a very pretty reaction.

Jayne wondered how many times Rachel had

practiced that. Way more than Jayne would ever have patience for.

Chris took another step forward, so he was even with Rachel. "I'll take your phone," he said to Jayne. "I'm sure the password is there."

Jayne shook her head. "It's not. I would never leave a password on my phone. That's what password managers are for. Want me to call Elmer and have him confirm?"

Chris shook his head. "No. Elmer isn't smart enough—"

"Stop right there," Jayne said. "No maligning my staff."

"They won't be your staff for long," Rachel said. "Not after word gets out that you let a big data breach happen on your watch. And you won't be able to find a new job, either."

Jayne crossed her arms across her chest. "What don't you like about me? You've had it in for me since I arrived."

Chris answered. "We didn't want anyone to be in charge of security," he said. "We were doing just fine without all your processes and procedures."

Now Jayne hoped Elmer was recording this. She continued, "So you could continue selling the company's secrets. And colluding with one of the investors to sell out all the others? Make a killing? Well, not a person, just with money."

Chris shook his head, his aftershave making her just a little queasy. Or, maybe it was that rollercoaster thing. He said, "Look, money is how we tell who's winning and who's losing. We—" and he looked at Rachel—"are winners. You are a loser."

Rachel said, "Hand over the master password. Now."

Jayne shrugged and said, "As I said before, that's not how it works."

"Chris," Rachel said, "Do something."

That's when Jayne heard sirens approaching. She watched as three police cars and at least two fire trucks entered the parking lot, all with lights and sirens.

She'd never been so happy to have a backdoor in Security Central.

"Hey, boss," Elmer said from her phone.

Chris looked at the door.

Rachel looked around.

"Yes, Elmer?" she said.

"I think you managed to trigger a full response."

Jayne finally relaxed a little and took a deep breath in. She promptly coughed due to the aftershave odor. "I think so. Let our fine police and fire people in the building, please."

"I think they didn't need me," he said.

That's when she heard footsteps pounding up the stairs.

An hour later, back in Security Central, Jayne took a deep breath in and let it out, finally sitting with a cup of green tea, its light jasmine odor inviting her to relax just a little. She was still cold in this room—she would never understand how her team liked it that cold.

The monitors at the top of the walls showed everything as clear.

She sat next to Elmer, who had finished his pizza and was now drinking water out of a giant insulated cup.

She and Elmer had debriefed with the cops, who had carted Chris and Rachel away in handcuffs.

Elmer finished typing something, his keystrokes calm, not angry. He finished with a flourish and turned to her.

"So," he said. "How did the cops and the fire people know to come here?"

She grinned. "As part of the backdoor, I added a few instructions so they would know to come. And I gave them a keycard so they could get into the building."

"And Chris and Rachel?" He shook his head. "She was so hot. I'll miss seeing her around."

Jayne laughed out loud. "I'm sure she'll be happy knowing you thought she was hot."

He shrugged.

"The cops took them away in handcuffs. I really hope I didn't smile, but I suspect I did."

Elmer shook his head. "They had it coming," he said, all trace of a smile gone. "They would have bankrupted us just for their private gain."

Jayne nodded and drank her tea. Her stomach started to growl, this time from hunger.

"How did they do it?" he asked.

"As far as I can tell, it's like most successful breaches—somebody gained physical access to the building. Remember that guy we interviewed a couple of months ago, who thought he was God's Gift to security?"

Elmer grinned. "I do remember. And I remember tripping him up on some relatively easy questions. If he'd been willing to learn, he would have been great. But he was not."

"Rachel got her claws into him. She hired him

—on the side—to try to break through our defenses. And of course, she gave him physical access to her account in her office."

Elmer shook his head. "Well, we can't stop senior leadership from doing stupid things."

"I'm thinking that maybe we can, but it will take some work."

Elmer paused. "So what do you do now?"

Jayne thought for a few seconds. "I think it's time for me to try my hand at running a company, not just security."

Elmer raised his eyebrows.

"That's actually why the investors hired me. They didn't trust Chris or Rachel. So I started in Security."

Elmer laughed. "You definitely flew under my radar!"

Jayne smiled. "Yes. A classic case of misdirection."

JUDGE, JURY, AND EXECUTIONER

JOSLYN CHASE

Traces of the storm that had rocked the Puget Sound all night still slicked the blacktop, raising tiny clouds of mist to hover over the pavement in the warmth of morning. It wasn't cold, yet Chief Steadman felt a chill feather along his spine as he steered the department's SUV onto the shoulder, pulling up behind an ambulance with lights still flashing.

"Holy smokes," Deputy Frost said from the passenger seat. His hands gripping the dashboard in front of him showed white around the knuckles and Steadman felt the same tension squeezing his insides.

"What on earth happened here?" he muttered.

A patrol car lay upside down, lodged against a stand of pines, exposing a gouged and tortured underbelly. One axle, wrenched away like a discarded limb, rested a full six yards from the vehicle. The body of the car was smashed almost beyond recognition.

Steadman hated to think how the body inside must look.

His stomach lurched, dropping like a broken elevator. Deputy Sarah Jenkins was a favorite of his, a sweet woman, quiet yet highly competent. An officer of sound judgement and a valuable member of the team, Steadman couldn't imagine how she'd ended up like this. The torn wreckage of a single car accident spoke of excessive speed and rash decisions.

That wasn't Sarah.

Wrenching open his door, Steadman climbed out and slammed it. The noise felt loud in the sober silence of emergency personnel moving zombie-like about their business, seeing to one of their own. He and Frost weren't the only ones operating in stunned disbelief.

Sheriff Polander stood next to a double furrow of churned grass and dirt showing the path the patrol car had taken to its death. His blue eyes, always a bit bulgy, now looked as if they might pop from their sockets. His face was a dull, mottled red as he clutched his uniform hat to his breast.

Steadman went to meet him, Frost at his side. "What the hell, Sheriff? Any chance Sarah might still be alive in there?"

Polander shook his head. "No, Chief. She's not." He hesitated, blinking his protruding eyes. "I'm sorry."

Frost took a step forward. "How did this happen?"

The sheriff dragged in a deep breath and gestured up the steep narrow country road with his hat. "Techs say she came from up there, going way too fast on the wet pavement. Took this curve, and it took her. Right down there to that row of evergreens."

Steadman scowled down at the ruined car. "She never had a chance."

Polander bowed his head. "No, she didn't."

"What can I do to help?" Steadman asked.

The sheriff's lips thinned as he pressed them together. "About all we can do is stay out of the way and let them do their work," he said, nodding to the emergency responders. "Sarah's beyond our help now."

"God bless her," Frost added.

Steadman watched the team move in with the hydraulic rescue tools known as the jaws of life, ironically named, in this case. He winced and looked away as they pulled Deputy Sarah Jenkins from the wreckage, waiting until they had her decently covered before turning back and making his way to where the medical examiner crouched over Sarah's remains.

Dr. Carolyn Neal rose as he approached, kneading the small of her back. Nearing retirement age, her movements were a little slower, a little stiffer, than they'd been when Steadman first met her, fifteen years ago.

The same could be said about him.

Her light brown hair, touched with gray and worn short, was hidden under a surgical cap. Her face shone pale beneath the blue. "Hell of a thing," she said in greeting.

"I'm still reeling," Steadman agreed. "Any insights into how this could have happened?"

Neal's nostrils flared slightly. "Alcohol-related."

Steadman felt the shock like a body slam. "No way," he said. "Sarah was not a drinker."

Frost piped up, indignation vibrating through his voice. "I never saw her take anything harder than a Shirley Temple."

"Are you sure, Carolyn?"

For answer, the doctor knelt and unzipped the body bag. The unmistakable odor of sour mash whiskey rose like vapor on the morning air.

"Was she alone in the car?" Steadman asked.

"There's no sign of anyone else. We've searched the area. She was alone," Neal confirmed. "And drinking hard."

Steadman thanked the M.E. and strode back to the SUV with Frost at his heels. Neither spoke until Steadman fired the engine.

"This is moronious," Frost said, using a term he'd morphed from the words moronic and erroneous, meaning both ridiculous and wrong.

"Moronious indeed," Steadman agreed. "Sarah

Jenkins was an exemplary officer and a fine human being." He put the car in gear and eased out onto the road.

"I intend to find out what really happened here."

The atmosphere back at the station felt stale and subdued, like Sarah's death had sucked some of the air from the room. Even Fred Winter, the sergeant manning the front desk, refrained from giving his usual "hang loose" greeting, the customary unsinkable smile missing from his face as Steadman filed past.

Frost scuffed along behind him as they crossed the open bull pen area. Most of the desks were empty and silence echoed through the space normally filled with the bustle of paperwork and phone talk. Steadman slowed as he neared Sarah's desk, glancing at the few heads bent over their work.

No one met his gaze and as he passed, he casually lifted a few file folders from the top of a stack on Sarah's desk and carried them to his office where Frost joined him.

"What's up, Chief?"

Steadman placed the folders on his blotter and sank into his chair, feeling it shift as it took his weight. "I'm entertaining a disturbing idea, Frost."

Frost looked unhappily at the folders. "You think her work had something to do with her death?"

"Given what I know about her and what I know about the Gibson case, I'd say that makes more sense than Sarah downing a bottle of whiskey and driving head on into a wall of Ponderosa pines."

"Are you suggesting her death wasn't an accident?"

Steadman chewed his lip, studying his partner. "What do you think? Got any gut feeling on this?"

Frost considered a moment, the crease between his brows deepening as he shook his head. "No, you're right. The scenario doesn't fit the Sarah I knew."

He paused. "But if there was something wrong with the car—if it had been tampered with—the crime scene techs will find out and let us know."

Steadman's heart sat like lead in his chest. He remembered his early days on the force, when he'd had such simple faith in the reliability of the justice system he worked for. Hard experience had trampled the shine off it, but he liked to believe the foundation was still there. He wanted to agree with Frost's assertion but said nothing instead.

"Won't they?" Frost pressed.

Steadman sighed and opened the top folder. "Normally, that would be true. But I have a bad feeling about this, Frost. Sarah was knee-deep into investigating the Gibson money laundering and fraud case."

Pausing to suck at a hangnail that had caught on the papers in the file, he continued, "The Gibsons are a powerful bunch in this county. How is it they've been able to get away with so much for so long?"

Frost frowned. "Inside help?"

"Gotta be." Steadman leaned forward and lowered his voice. "Last week I ran into Sarah at the coffee stand on the corner. She told me—in confidence—that she was starting an investigation into Judge Holloway."

"What?"

Frost's jaw dropped, exposing the glint of a filling at the back of his mouth. "Judge Edward Holloway is the most respected judge in the county. He's been on the bench longer than anyone else."

Steadman rubbed a hand over his forehead. "Sad prospect, isn't it?" He pointed to a note in the margin of a crime report in Sarah's file. "But it looks like she found something to back up her suspicions."

He showed Frost four or five places where Sarah had marked the initials "JH" against charges she was investigating. JH, for Judge Holloway.

Frost pushed back from the desk. "But it's not really proof, is it? Just her ideas. I can't believe Judge Holloway would be mixed up in a crime conspiracy."

Steadman smiled. He liked his partner and admired his moral fortitude. "If all lawmen were like you, Frost, I wouldn't believe it either. It pains me to say that Sarah may have been onto something big and that may have been what got her killed."

Frost blew out a long breath, his face darkening with a scowl. "And that's what drove her to drink? No pun intended, Chief, but I find that hard to swallow."

"So do I. In point of fact, I don't believe she did drink that whiskey," Steadman said.

He paused, allowing his hands to clench in his lap.

"I believe someone poured it down her throat."

When Quinn Jenkins answered the doorbell, Steadman felt a tug at his gut. The man's face was pale enough to fade into a snowbank and, emotionally speaking, that might be exactly where he was.

Steadman didn't know how to help him through that, but he wanted Sarah's husband to know that he wasn't alone in his grief. Or alone in feeling the loss of someone very special.

Placing a hand on Quinn's shoulder, he said, "I'm so sorry. We all loved Sarah." He paused, swallowing. "We'll all miss her."

Frost gripped the man's hand and murmured, "Sorry for your loss."

Quinn Jenkins stepped back, gesturing vaguely toward the living room. Steadman wiped his feet on the mat and entered. He'd been there on a few previous occasions—a backyard barbecue, coffee after attending a play at the high school, and once for a friendly game of Spades.

Quinn collapsed into an armchair and Steadman took that for a silent invitation to be seated. He and Frost settled onto the sofa and Steadman placed a tray of homemade pastries on the coffee table.

"Vivi remembered how much you liked her cinnamon rolls," he told Quinn. He recalled the words Quinn had said at the time—"My favorite comfort food." He hoped the rolls might bring some comfort now.

But it wouldn't be nearly enough.

"This is not an official visit, Quinn," Steadman said. "We just wanted to drop by and let you know we stand ready to help however we can."

He let a beat pass. "And to let you talk. Sometimes it's a relief just to talk and know someone is listening."

Quinn nodded but said nothing. Steadman let his gaze wander around the room, taking in the familiar furniture, just waiting for Quinn's dam to break. His eyes rested on a new item that hadn't been there before, and his blood ran cold. He stared, new grief curdling within him.

"It's not what you think," Quinn said.

Steadman realized the bereaved man had seen him gaping at the baby carriage and the stuffed bunny peeping over the rim. He must have known the conclusion Steadman would draw from it.

"Sarah wasn't pregnant," Quinn said quietly.

After a second, he opened his mouth to say something more, but only a hoarse single syllable came out. Clearing his throat, he spoke again. "We had just decided to start trying. Sarah's mom…" His voice dwindled into helpless silence.

Steadman understood what he meant. His own

mother-in-law had been euphoric at the prospect of her first grandchild, showering them with all kinds of goodies in expectation. On the sofa next to him, Frost covered a cough, using it as an excuse to take a quick swipe at his eyes.

Once the ball was rolling, Quinn kept talking, letting his grief spill out in drips and gushes, mostly what Steadman expected to hear until he said, "She was afraid, you know."

A pause. "In those last couple of days, I think she was afraid for her life."

"What makes you think that?" Steadman asked.

Quinn pressed his fingers against his forehead, working to get control. Finally, he said, "I should have done something. I should have taken it more seriously."

"Don't do this," Frost said. "You are not responsible for what happened."

"Don't shoulder that burden," Steadman agreed. "You've got enough on your shoulders right now for anyone." He waited a decent second before adding, "Did Sarah tell you something?"

"She said she found something rotten, something explosive."

"She didn't say what it was or who it concerned?"

Quinn shook his head. "No. I'm sorry. She said

she wasn't a hundred percent certain and sterling reputations were at stake. That's how she phrased it."

"But you have no idea who she meant?"

"Only that it must be someone high up the ladder."

"Any idea which ladder?"

"No."

As Steadman left the house with Frost, his determination to uncover the truth behind the death of Sarah Jenkins shone brighter than ever, almost burning a hole through his chest.

As they climbed into the SUV, Frost said, "As I see it, we have two important decisions to make upfront. How far are we willing to take this? And are we taking Lily with us?"

Steadman buckled his seat belt. "All the way, and hell no."

Lily Jamieson was a fellow deputy and a valuable resource, excellent at digging up information and tracking down leads. She was also especially dear to Frost's heart.

Snapping his own belt into place, Frost said, "Good. We're in agreement on both counts. We're doing this, and we're keeping Lily in the dark."

"We're keeping everyone in the dark. Anyone who might find out we're poking into Sarah's 'accident' is either on the wrong side of the line or someone we're putting in danger."

"I think you pegged it, Chief," Frost said, sighing.

As Steadman headed the car back toward the station, he said, "You realize, of course, that Lily will not thank us for leaving her out of this."

"No, she won't," Frost said, sounding forlorn. "She'll be mad as a hornet in a hailstorm when she finds out, but that's a risk I'm willing to take if it will keep her out of harm's way."

Steadman tightened his hands on the steering wheel. "I just hope it will."

Steadman massaged behind his ears where a tension headache sprouted, sending out tendrils. He lifted the cup at his elbow and swirled the dregs of cold coffee, grimacing at the bitter scent that hovered like an echo of the sting in his gut.

Without Lily's help, he and Frost had made slow progress over the two days since Sarah's death, discreetly sandwiching their probing efforts between official business, careful not to set off any alarms.

But not careful enough.

After uncovering a series of financial discrepancies linked to Judge Holloway's rulings, and payments connected to a major fraud case involving a local businessman, an anonymous text message popped up on the screen of Steadman's cell phone:

Fingers that poke often get broke. Stop.

"We hit a sore spot," Frost said.

"Sure looks like we found the right tree," Steadman agreed. "But shaking it is liable to be hazardous to our health."

"We've got to shake it, boss. We can't just let that rot grow and spread to the whole orchard."

Steadman regarded Frost's determined glare, the way his palms were planted, flat and emphatic, on the desktop. Such freedom from political ambiguity was a luxury Steadman no longer enjoyed. He envied his partner, but he also feared for him.

And for himself.

"Let's take a step back and think about this," Steadman said. "I want to find out what happened to Sarah as much as you do, but with something this dark, more than our jobs could be at stake."

He paused. "I have a wife, children, one sweet grandbaby and another on the way."

Frost blanched. He pushed back from the desk. "You don't think Holloway would threaten your family, do you?"

"Holloway. The Gibsons. Dangerous people, Frost. I have to consider it, and so should you."

"Are you suggesting we back down?"

Steadman sighed. "I'm suggesting we make it *look* like we're dropping it cold."

"And what are we really doing, Chief?"

"We're calling an old friend for help."

Steadman rested his arms on the round poker table in Garth Rafferty's basement game room. He regarded his friend across the green baize of the table as Frost, seated next to him, fiddled with a stack of five-dollar chips.

A year ago, this is where Garth had schooled him in the art of poker and reading people. Steadman had always been a good interrogator, expertly picking up on micro expressions and nonverbal cues, but he'd learned the hard way that his skills didn't necessarily transfer to the poker table.

Garth had worked with him to bridge the gap, yet their combined efforts hadn't been enough, in light of the challenge Steadman faced and the danger it posed to his sister and her husband.

Together with Frost and Lily, he and Garth had faced down a monster and lived to tell the tale, so he knew Garth had the guts and the brains. But would he muster the will to tackle another poisonous beast?

Ten years retired, Garth spent his days sporting Hawaiian shirts and playing penny ante poker with a couple cronies in the neighborhood. In his working days, he'd had Steadman's job and was a legend in the department, having solved more cases than anyone else in the city's history and putting away a slew of vile lawbreakers.

Steadman was willing to bet he still had connections and back door entry into a variety of data fortresses. Exactly the kind of access they would need to keep their investigation on the down low.

And Steadman held an ace up his sleeve—Garth had a sizeable soft spot in his heart for Deputy Sarah Jenkins. He'd want a big slice of serving up justice if her death proved to be more than what it appeared on the surface.

As was his habit, Garth held a wooden toothpick between his teeth, gnawing it to splinters. It bobbed as he spoke. "Does the sheriff know what you're up to, Steadman?"

"Somebody knows," Frost said. "They sent chief a nastygram."

"Is that right?"

"Threatened to break a finger if I didn't lay off."

"Uh-huh."

Garth glowered. Frost scowled. They all knew the broken finger was code for something much worse.

"I showed Sheriff Polander the text message, told him I entertained a few doubts about the manner of Sarah's death, and mentioned the margin notations in Sarah's case file."

Garth leaned forward. "What did he say?"

"He looked genuinely shocked that anyone would suspect Judge Holloway of wrongdoing. He assured me there could be no grounds for my suspicions and that I'd be the first to know if anything turned up. He asked that I return the files I took from Sarah's desk."

"And did you?"

"Yes, of course. I even managed to look a little shame-faced as I handed them over."

"You made copies?"

"Every last page, and I pulled all the Post-it notes she had attached and kept those for us."

"So, we're going completely covert on this?" Garth asked.

Steadman smiled. "Does that mean you're in?"

"Hell yes, I'm in." He pulled the toothpick

from between his lips and surveyed its shattered line before tossing it into a cut-glass ashtray filled with soggy wooden shards.

"You sure know how to buff the dull off a man's retirement, Steadman."

He pushed away from the table and stretched his arms, straining the buttons on his palm tree-printed shirt.

"Let's get to work."

In the parking lot of an upscale bar called Smitty's, Steadman sat behind the wheel of a dark blue Ford. The car was a rental, one which Garth had assured him would keep them anonymous for at least 48 hours.

Which meant they were walking on a tightrope, with a candle burning the wire on both ends.

He hunched down as a car turned into the lot, its headlights sweeping across the rows of vehicles like a probing finger. In the seat next to him, Frost ducked his own head to the side, bringing it within bumping distance. Steadman smelled chocolate milkshake on his breath and straightened his spine.

"Crack a window, Frost. It's getting stuffy in here."

"Sure thing, boss."

They'd left Garth in his basement, stacks of paper and computer monitors spread out along the wet bar as he tapped at his keyboard like a woodpecker on pine. In a little under three hours, he'd uncovered a number of dubious connections and suspicious payouts that could be traced back to Holloway associates, though less definitively to the man himself.

Taking one of those names—a man called Ramsauer—Steadman and Frost had staked out his house and followed him to this bar. Since going inside posed too great a risk of being recognized, they watched Ramsauer through the murky window as he spoke with another man. An unknown.

They aimed to find out who he was and if he could be connected to Holloway or the Gibson clan.

"Here he comes," Frost said, lowering his window further to get a good shot with the camera. He snapped a series of photos as the man crossed to a classic-style white Corvette and climbed inside.

"Garth ought to be able to do something with those," Steadman said.

"Are we going to tail him? See where he goes?"

"You bet."

Steadman waited until the Corvette left the parking lot, turning right, before starting the engine and following at a distance. The white car shone under the streetlights, making it easy to keep in sight until they passed out of the downtown area into the darker, wooded spaces outside the city limits.

The Corvette slowed and made the turn into an upscale, quiet neighborhood with expensive houses on generous lots. Steadman felt a chill scurry down his spine.

"This is where Holloway lives," he said.

Taking his foot off the accelerator, he let the Ford coast to a crawl as the Corvette veered left onto Holloway's street, about a hundred yards ahead.

"We need to get photo evidence of this guy's connection to Holloway," Frost said. "Hurry, or we'll miss him going in."

"How many cars do you see cruising these streets, Frost? We come in too close, too soon, and we get made."

"So what do we do?"

"We park in a nice shady spot where the car won't be noticed, and we move in on foot. We conceal ourselves and we wait. Catch him on the way out."

"That could take all night."

"It could," Steadman agreed.

He found a darkened driveway about a quarter mile short of Holloway's house. No lights shone in the windows and a realtor's sign hung on a post in the front yard, so Steadman didn't anticipate any complaints about using the spot.

By the time he and Frost reached the Holloway property on foot, the Corvette parked on the circular drive was empty, the door of the house firmly closed. They found a place to hunker down behind a hedge bordering the property line. From here, Frost ought to be able to capture some good photos of the man leaving Holloway's residence.

"Does the judge have dogs?" Frost asked, a hint of worry in his voice.

"He strikes me as more of a cat person," Steadman said. "But I could be wrong."

Inch by inch, the rising moon escaped the grasp of the overhead tree branches, coming into full view between the gently waving boughs. Crickets chirped and a dog barked in the distance but otherwise, the night was calm and quiet.

Like before a storm.

By the time the front door of Holloway's house opened again, Steadman's legs were shooting pins and needles and his back ached from the prolonged crouching.

He exhaled the tension of waiting and inhaled a big breath of new anxiety as motion-activated floodlights painted a bright swath across the lawn, probing into the hidey hole he shared with Frost.

Feeling like a bug pinned to a display board, Steadman squinted against the bright lights but was relieved to see that none of the three men gathered around the Corvette bothered looking in their direction.

A twinge of gratification brought a smile to his lips as a ginger-colored cat slinked from the doorway to curl around Judge Holloway's trousered legs. Kneeling in the bushes beside him, Frost worked the camera from a variety of angles, documenting this meeting of Holloway and the two mystery men.

Steadman hoped the result would be worth the risk.

Cricket song had ceased with the sudden spill of light and Steadman heard the mens' voices but couldn't make out their words. By their tone, they were saying their parting lines, but the hair on the back of his neck stiffened as one of them gave a guttural shout.

"Hey! You, behind the bushes, come out!"

Steadman didn't hesitate. In an instant, he was pelting across the neighbor's lawn with Frost streaking along beside him. Footsteps pounded in their wake and the Corvette's motor roared to life.

Cutting through the backyard, Steadman found an alleyway and sprinted twenty yards before ducking into a half-open gateway with Frost following like an electrified shadow. He eased the gate shut behind them, heart thumping in his chest. With one pursuer dogging them on foot and the Corvette patrolling the road out front, he felt an alarming kinship with the hunted fox.

But darkness was their friend.

Halting and doing his best to melt into the trees beside a toolshed, Steadman drew a deep breath through his nose and pursed his lips, controlling the air as it escaped his lungs, keeping it quiet.

Frost, younger and more fit, inhaled and exhaled with open mouth, nearly inaudible as they molded themselves to the tree trunks. The sounds of pursuit neared their location and Steadman's pulse ratcheted up a notch, nearly stopping when the footsteps fell silent, not five yards from where he stood.

Tight as a bowstring about to snap, he strained his ears to detect movement, but only the whisper of a breeze came to him on the night air. He waited a whole minute, and then two. Beside him, he sensed Frost about to move or speak and put a warning hand on his partner's shoulder.

Another minute passed and then a resigned sigh from the alleyway accompanied the thud of boots on hard-packed dirt as their pursuer moved on. Quivering with the adrenaline rush, Steadman continued to listen as the footsteps faded into the distance.

He debated whether it was wiser to move out or stay put. Movement increased the risk of being seen or heard but it cut against the grain to stand and do nothing. What if the man came back with a flashlight for a closer look?

"I'm itching to get out of here," Frost said, his voice a fervent whisper.

Steadman felt the same. "Let's do it," he agreed. "Before they decide to lock down the area."

Within five minutes, he was popping the door locks on the Ford. The street looked deserted, houses dark and shuttered for the night as he climbed behind the wheel.

"It's two o'clock in the morning," Frost said. "They'll be all over any car that moves."

Steadman started the engine and let off the hand brake. "I'd bet a month's wages the Corvette is sitting on the main road, covering both exits from the neighborhood."

"And they're sure to have at least one more backup car roving the streets. What do we do?"

"It so happens," Steadman said as he rolled out of the driveway, headlights off, "that I know a back way. An old fire road we had to use a dozen summers ago when a blaze broke out on the ridge above."

He drove fast, straining his eyes in the gloom, reluctant to activate the headlights and call attention their way. Turning toward the rear section of the winding roads dotted with houses, Steadman found he was holding his breath and let it out in a *whoosh*, feeling some of his tension loosen and go with it.

At the end of a cul-de-sac, he slowed the Ford and nosed it onto a rutted lane. Even at a crawl, it took less than ten seconds before the woodland looming above Holloway's neighborhood swallowed them whole.

But the darkness that hid them also made it impossible to continue very far down the narrow poorly maintained track. Though the mass of pines and birch seemed thick, Steadman knew it wouldn't reliably mask the headlights if he switched them on. He'd be giving their pursuers a homing beacon as they moved across the ridge above the spread of houses.

The car gave a lurch accompanied by a hideous scraping noise as it wandered off the road. Steadman wrestled the wheel and corrected their course but after another slow and treacherous fifty yards, the Ford bounced and came to rest against something solid. He cut the engine and peered at Frost through the murk.

"What do we do now?" his partner asked.

"We've got three hours 'til sunrise. Best case scenario, they'll think we got away before they closed the net. We wait for Mother Nature to light the way and get on out of here."

Frost cleared his throat. "And worst case?"

"Worst case, they start coming up this road. That's when we switch on the headlights, make a run for it, and hope like hell they don't cut us off at the pass."

Next morning, Steadman and Frost arrived separately at the station as if nothing out of the ordinary had occurred the night before.

As if they hadn't spent a tense three hours listening for the sound of a laboring engine sneaking up on them in the dark. Or peering into the inky shadows for signs of movement.

As if they hadn't bumped over a rough forest path to emerge on a dirt road in the pale light of dawn before hiding the dust-plastered Ford in Garth's garage and returning home for a quick cleanup and change of clothes.

Despite the steaming shower and an even hotter pot of strong coffee served up with a plate of scrambled eggs and toast by his worried-looking wife, Steadman felt a hollow sense of dread. They'd been foolish to think they could move quietly in the background, unnoticed.

There'd be hell to pay.

Lily entered the bull pen, giving Frost a secret smile as she passed them and slid in behind her desk. Steadman caught a whiff of orange blossom shampoo and figured his partner was probably halfway to getting drunk on the scent.

"What kind of mischief have the two of you been spinning?" Lily asked.

Frost's head popped up like a groundhog checking his shadow. "What? No mischief here," he said. "What makes you ask?"

Lily narrowed her eyes, suspicion lifting the

corners of her lovely brows. "Polander wants to see you in his office," she said. "That's why I'm asking. Sounds like trouble."

"Nah," Steadman assured her, hoping to lay her curiosity to rest. "He just wants an update on a case we're working."

Lily studied him. "Uh-huh."

She didn't sound convinced.

A variety-pack of misgivings reared in Steadman's mind as he and Frost filed into the sheriff's inner sanctum. The protruding blue eyes regarded Frost with melancholy as he motioned them into chairs set before the large oak desk cluttered with stacks of paperwork.

"I must say, I'm disappointed, Deputy Frost. I wouldn't have believed you were the type."

"The type for what?" Steadman asked.

Polander's sorrowful gaze shifted to Steadman. "I hope you weren't a part of this, Chief."

"A part of what?" Steadman repeated, keeping his voice even.

The sheriff shook his head. "Like I said, I would never have believed it without a stack of corroborating evidence, but here it is."

He opened a file folder in front of him and began paging through the contents. "Greg over in Property brought this to my attention this morning. I've been going over it for the last hour and Deputy Frost, I'm sorry—I have no choice but to suspend you pending further investigation."

"Further investigation of what?" Steadman said, working very hard to keep firm control of his voice.

Frost sat stunned in his chair and Steadman felt a knife forged of wrath and bitterness slice through him. Frost was the most moral man he knew, a man who cherished integrity in others and nurtured it tirelessly in himself.

All color gone from his face, Frost said, "What am I being accused of, Sheriff?"

"Now, Deputy, I think you know the answer to that. Otherwise, we wouldn't be having this conversation."

"He certainly doesn't know," Steadman said. He leaned forward and pinned the sheriff with a grim stare. "Otherwise, we wouldn't be having this conversation."

"Now, Chief, I know he's your partner and all, and I understand—"

"You understand nothing, Sheriff, if you think Cory Frost knowingly broke the law or violated the standards of his office."

Polander's blue stare cooled a degree as he met Steadman's gaze. "Currently, I have no reason to believe you were involved with Deputy Frost's questionable activities." He paused. "You may go."

Steadman didn't move. "What 'questionable activities' is Deputy Frost supposedly involved in?"

Spots of color, pink and feverish, rose high on Frost's cheeks but his voice came out strong and unafraid. "What are you claiming I did?" he asked the sheriff. "I have a right to know what I'm being accused of."

Polander's bulging eyes glared at Frost, his lips curling in disdain. "Evidence tampering," he said. "These records indicate that you manipulated and misappropriated evidence in at least two cases during the last year."

"I did not," Frost said, indignation quivering in his voice.

Steadman flashed him a warning look and when he continued, his words were steady and even-toned. "I have never, at any time, manipulated, removed, or tampered with evidence."

"We'll see," Polander responded. "Like I said, there will be an investigation. In the meantime, you're suspended. I want you out of the building in the next ten minutes."

"Sheriff, I—"

Polander held up a hand, palm out, cutting him off. "Tell it to the jury, Frost. You are dismissed."

He turned to Steadman, his blotchy complexion a dull, glowering red. "Back to work for you. I want those incident reports on my desk by close of business today."

He strode across to his private attached bathroom and closed the door with a sharp snap, leaving Steadman and Frost to deal with the shock he'd delivered. Steadman stepped to the oak desk and quickly studied the files Frost had allegedly tampered with.

"It's all bunk," Frost said.

"Bunk," Steadman agreed, "but it appears to be well-substantiated bunk."

The color had again faded from Frost's features. Steadman tightened his fists and straightened from Polander's desk.

"I swear I will do everything I can to get you out of this, Frost. We'll get through it and see clear skies again on the other side."

"I know we will," Frost said quietly.

He left the office and Steadman followed, tension pulsing through him as he poised to face the questions Lily was sure to launch at them. Relief flooded over him when he saw her desk standing empty and no sign of her in the corridor. He and Frost exchanged a glance as his partner hastily gathered a few items from his desk before they hurried to the parking garage.

"Let's meet at Garth's tonight," Steadman said as Frost beeped open the door of his Nissan Sentra. "We can figure out where to go from here."

"Sure."

Steadman summoned a smile. "Vivi told me she's baking cookies today. I'll bring some."

Cookies. As if that would solve everything.

"I like cookies," Frost said. "Especially Vivi's."

He climbed into the car and paused before slamming the door. "Thanks, chief. It's going to be okay. We'll come out on top."

Steadman gave a firm nod of agreement and watched the Sentra as it left the parking area. Turning, he headed for the stairwell and was startled to see three shadowy shapes materialize from a dark corner of the garage, cutting off his path to the stairs.

Like a bank of thunderclouds, they swept toward him.

Two of the men, clad in black leather jackets and jeans, had faces Steadman didn't recognize. The third man was the one he and Frost had followed to Holloway's place on the previous evening. The driver of the white Corvette.

They stopped three yards in front of him and

stood, legs spread like sailors on a shifting deck. The Corvette guy took another step forward and the mocking smile on his lips made Steadman itch to plow a fist into it.

"Looks like you got a dirty partner, Chief Steadman."

Steadman gritted his teeth and said nothing.

"The way I hear it, he's headed toward an arrest if any more evidence turns up. He'll be finished as an officer of the law."

Leading with one shoulder, like a quarterback carrying the ball, Steadman moved to break through their line. "If you'll excuse me, I have work to do," he said.

The two unknowns grabbed him and Corvette, now behind him, delivered a quick punch to the kidneys.

"We won't hold you up much longer," he said, speaking directly into Steadman's ear, the hiss of hot breath raising the hairs at the nape of his neck as pain from his kidneys washed over him. "Just wanted to make sure you got this memo—your boy scout partner, your sweet lady wife, your kiddies and grandbabies will all thank you to let this go, Steadman."

One of the other goons spoke up. "It sure

would be a shame if something happened to any one of them."

A wave of acid fought its way up from Steadman's stomach, burning in his throat. He spun under Corvette's arm and the thugs let him go, shouting a few choice phrases at his retreating back. Breathing fast, heart thundering behind his ribs, Steadman rushed to his own car, forsaking the stairs and the stack of incident reports on his desk.

He had to get home.

"Shoot!" Frost said. "This is beyond moronious."

They were back in Garth's basement, seated around the poker table with not a chip in sight. Steadman, still out of breath, pulse beating hard in his chest after a whirlwind of preparations, sprawled in his chair and tried to ignore the soreness in the small of his back.

He'd helped Vivi collect their pregnant daughter, along with their daughter-in-law and four-year-old grandchild, sending them to a pre-arranged safe location. They had all been drilled for this and had bugout bags and a cash stash at the ready. But it had been natural disasters—Mt. Rainier erupting or a major earthquake—that they'd expected to be escaping.

Not the claws of human monsters.

"Yes," Garth agreed. "Moronious doesn't begin to cover it. Diabolical, wicked, unconscionable, all come a little closer."

"You might want to distance yourself from the fallout, Garth," Steadman warned. "We can figure out a way to do this without you."

"Like hell you will. Remember that witness who was gunned down before he could testify against the Gibsons last year? I traced a wire transfer to the shooter, handled by a bank in the Caymans. From there, twenty million in Swedish krona was wired from a secure family trust."

"Did you get the name of the family?"

"I had to break through some shells, but I'll give you one guess what I came up with."

"Gibson."

"Correct. I've got printouts of evidence that ought to put every one of these crooks behind bars."

"Provided we can find a judge who'll pay them any credence," Steadman pointed out. "We don't know who we can go to."

"What about Polander? Is he on the up or just another arm of the monster?"

Steadman replayed the scene in the sheriff's office, remembering the look on Polander's face.

"Either he really believes Frost is guilty of evidence tampering or he's a damn fine actor," he said, huffing out a frustrated sigh. "I can't really say which side he's supporting."

"That's a shame," Garth said, "and here's some more bad news. Holloway's allies in the legal system are shutting down leads, closing off avenues. I'll bet if I went back to where I got half this stuff, it would be erased by now as if it never existed. We might all go down for evidence tampering in the end."

"All for one, and one for all," Frost said, but his voice was tinged with sarcasm rather than determination. Steadman found that as scary as anything that had happened so far.

Straightening in his chair, he opened his mouth to speak but urgent vibrations from the phone in his pocket pre-empted what he'd been going to say.

"Chief Steadman, this is Sheriff Polander. If you know where your buddy Frost is, please encourage him to come down to the station. We have a warrant for his arrest."

The silence of the empty house fell on Steadman's eardrums like a monotonous tolling bell. He hated the feel of the place without Vivi to warm it and keep it alive.

But he was too tense for music. Anything he played would only irritate him and besides, he wanted to be able to hear any slight noise that sounded out of place. He knew he was being paranoid but under the circumstances, there was no other way to be.

While he and Frost were sitting in Garth's basement, officers had executed a search warrant on Frost's apartment and confiscated several items stolen from the station's secure evidence locker. Rather than fan the intensifying flames, Frost had turned himself in, clinging to the shreds of his faith in a justice system he'd always revered.

Steadman's partner was spending the night in a jail cell. And if he couldn't find a way to clear Frost, it would be just the first of many. Filling a glass from the tap, Steadman swirled the water, watching it slosh over the sides and splash into the sink before he chugged what was left.

The cell phone on the counter beside him buzzed and he ignored it. Lily. She'd been trying to reach him for the past hour, and he didn't know what to say to her, how to explain or soothe the anxiety she had to be feeling. He needed to find a sliver of hope or encouragement to offer, but he had no idea where to look.

Letting out a snarl of frustration, Steadman hammered his fists down on the kitchen countertop, scattering the copied papers from the files Sarah had been working on before her death. Some of the pages drifted to the floor like oversized snowflakes and Steadman bent to collect them.

As he returned the papers to the folder, he caught sight of a doodle Sarah had drawn on a Post-it note attached to one sheet. A baby's rattle.

An ache swelled in his throat as he thought about what a wonderful mother Sarah would have been. Her child would assuredly have made valuable contributions to the world, contributions that now would never be.

He cleared his throat and traced his finger along the small slip of yellow paper where Sarah had scrawled the lines of a nursery rhyme, one he remembered from his own childhood. Sarah had modified it to suit herself.

Bye, baby bunting,
Mama's gone a-hunting,
Gone to get a rabbit skin
To wrap my little secret in.

A chill prickled over Steadman's scalp, freezing

him as he bent over the counter, staring at the scribbled words. He remembered the baby carriage in Sarah's living room and the lop-eared bunny that had peered at him over the rim.

Hope and amazement swelled within him as that rabbit took on new meaning. Grabbing his car keys and wallet, Steadman snagged a jacket off a peg by the front door and hurried to his car parked in the driveway.

His heart plummeted as he crossed the lawn. Even in the dim light cast by a distant streetlamp, he saw the bad news clearly.

All four tires were slashed.

Cool night air streamed over Steadman as he gunned the Harley's engine, speeding it down the road leading to Sarah's address. He leaned into a curve, remembering the feel of riding although it had been years since he'd been on a bike.

The Sportster belonged to Jim Peters, a neighbor three doors down. After taking in the tire situation, Steadman had crept through his own backyard and stolen across lawns and over fences to Jim's house. His friend had been happy to loan him the motorcycle, along with helmet and leather jacket, no questions asked.

The bike made a lot of noise and there'd be no disguising his arrival at Sarah's house. He hoped Quinn was still awake and willing to receive a night visitor with a strange request.

Steadman saw the curtains move in an upstairs window as he parked the Harley in the driveway. Not wanting to spook Sarah's husband or be shot on sight, he removed the helmet and left it with the bike, moving toward the front door with his empty hands in plain sight.

Quinn had reason to be fearful and Steadman wanted to ease that fear, not add to it. The door opened.

"Good evening, Quinn."

"Steadman?" The man squinted against the porch light, then beckoned him in. "I'm guessing this is no casual visit. What's going on?"

Quinn wore blue plaid pajamas beneath a black terry cloth robe belted at the waist. Steadman followed him inside and waited until he secured the door behind them. "This is a hell of a thing to ask," he said, "but do you still have the baby carriage?"

Quinn stared. "What? I mean, yes. I haven't thought about—"

"And the bunny?"

A sudden stab of foreboding jolted through Steadman, overriding his good manners. He pushed past Quinn into the living room and stopped halfway across the floor.

The rabbit was gone.

"What happened to the bunny?" Steadman asked, disappointment flooding over him.

Quinn's forehead furrowed and it seemed an age before he finally said, "I bagged it up with some other baby things I was going to give to my sister."

Steadman's knees went weak. He sank onto the sofa. "But it's still here? You still have it?"

"Yes. Why?"

Steadman let a beat pass while he pulled in a deep breath and let it out slow. "I think Sarah may have hidden something inside the rabbit. Her findings from the investigation. Evidence."

Quinn dropped into the chair next to him. "You mean a way to figure out the people who killed her?"

"And nail them."

Quinn reached into the space between sofa and chair and pulled forth a white plastic garbage bag with yellow drawstrings. He loosened them but seemed unable to move any further, overcome by a mix of emotions Steadman fervently hoped he'd never have to suffer.

Taking the bag from him, Steadman retrieved the stuffed rabbit, running his fingers over the seams until he encountered something stiff beneath the plush fabric. Examining the seam carefully, he saw that about an inch of it was sewn with thread of a slightly different shade from the rest.

Using his pocketknife, he cut the stitches, opening a gap to expose the fluffy white stuffing. And something small, square, and black.

A data storage chip.

Holding it between his fingers, Steadman looked wonderingly up at Quinn and met, instead, the hollow eye of a gun barrel.

A spurt of shock sizzled through Steadman's veins. He hadn't seen this coming but maybe he should have. Holloway's evil roots ran deep.

Quinn stood about five feet in front of him, the gun shaking a little in his hand. Steadman hoped it didn't have a hair trigger. Despite his trembling, Quinn's face was grim and determined, his shoulders squared beneath the black robe.

"I need that chip, Steadman. Give it here."

He extended his left hand, palm open, but Steadman didn't move. Five seconds ticked by before Quinn jabbed the gun forward. "Now," he shouted. "Give me the chip."

"Why?"

Quinn looked stricken. "It doesn't matter why." He paused and his voice took on a bleak tone. "I need that chip."

"Who did they threaten?" Steadman asked, thinking about the trio in the parking garage. "Your sister?"

A faint, desolate moan escaped Quinn's throat like a wisp of smoke. He nodded. "My sister and her two little kids. A three-year-old and a newborn, Steadman. I'm not going to let those bastards hurt them."

"Of course you're not."

Despite the hopeless tone of his words, Quinn's stance had not relaxed. He continued to hold the gun pointed determinedly in Steadman's direction, intent on taking possession of the data chip.

Steadman still held the pocketknife he'd used to slice through the rabbit's stitching. He felt the cold blade beneath his fingers and weighed his chances against Quinn and the gun. Reluctance pressed down on him like a millstone.

"They threatened to drown Carla's babies and make it look like she did it. She'd go to prison, branded as a child killer. Just like they branded

Sarah as a drunk driver before they murdered her."

The gun wavered in Quinn's hand as he choked back a sob. Steadman saw the muscles in his jaw clench. "Then they said they'd come for me."

Quinn took half a step forward, leading with the gun now held steady, aimed at Steadman's head.

"I've been searching Sarah's office," he said. "Sifting through every scrap of paper and every possible hiding spot." He gave a strangled cry. "I never thought to look inside a stuffed animal, a toy my own child will never play with."

Steadman stood. "I know you're hurting, Quinn, and I know you're scared. But you don't want to shoot me, and I don't believe you will."

He began moving toward the entry hall, but Quinn stepped to block him. "You better believe it, Steadman. I don't want to, but I will shoot you if that's what it takes to get that chip."

Slowly, carefully, Steadman showed him the pocketknife as he folded it and put it away. He held his hands open at his sides as he took another step toward the front hall.

"I'm walking out that door, Quinn," he said, "and here's why you're going to let me do it—because it's what Sarah would have wanted. She went through an awful lot of trouble to track down this evidence and protect it from people who want it destroyed. She gave her life for that cause. If all her efforts and her sacrifice go in vain, then she died for nothing."

Quinn stared, anguish and despair blooming in his face. His lips curled in a painful grimace and Steadman could almost smell the agony and desperation seeping from his pores.

With a frustrated growl, he threw the gun onto the sofa and raked his fingers through his hair. Steadman gripped him by the shoulders. Hard.

"We are going to stop them, Quinn."

"Damn right, we are," Garth said, stepping in from the kitchen.

Steadman's head jerked up in surprise. "What in blazes? How did you—? How long have you been standing there, Rafferty?"

He looked over Garth's shoulder and saw the broken pane in the kitchen door where Garth had done his breaking and entering.

"Long enough to give my antiperspirant a rigorous test drive. I was hoping I wouldn't have to shoot this guy," he said, pointing to Quinn.

"Can we all agree to limit our shooting to the bad guys?" Steadman said. "Quinn's with us. Am I right, Quinn?"

Steadman fixed his gaze on Sarah's husband and

what he saw there let him relax a notch or two. They had a new ally.

"And I brought someone else with me," Garth said. "To add to our list of assets."

He motioned toward the kitchen and Steadman watched Lily step from the shadows, the peeved look on her face telling him they'd be having words together sometime very soon.

Steadman drew in a deep breath, taking a moment to relax his muscles and just enjoy the rich aroma of strong coffee brewing. Quinn had changed out of his pajamas and the four of them sat around the kitchen table, facing the task of figuring out how to move forward on the perilous path before them.

"Sorry about your window," Garth said, indicating the shards of glass littering the tiles by the door. "I needed a quick and stealthy way in."

"Let me sweep that up for you," Lily said, rising and pulling a broom and dustpan from beside the refrigerator.

"How did you know to come here?" Steadman asked.

"It was Lily," Garth said. "She came to my place, pissed off as a sack of wet cats."

"As I have every right to be!" Lily said, stabbing the kitchen floor with the broom . "You should have told me what was going on. I am capable of helping, you know."

"No one knows it better, I assure you," Steadman told her. "We are dealing with a ruthless gang of thugs and their well-placed partners in high places. We wanted to…" He trailed off, not sure how to proceed without raising her dander to a whole new level.

"You wanted to protect me," she pitched in, pausing the broom to give him a meaningful glance. "I get that, and don't think it goes unappreciated. But I'm a big girl, Chief. A trained officer of the law, just like you."

Steadman smiled and held his hands out to her, palms up. "I'm sorry, Lily. Frost—"

"Ooh, that man! I went to see him in the holding cell, but he wouldn't tell me anything. That's why I turned to Garth."

"And it's a good thing she did," Garth added. "She's the one who figured it out."

"Figured what out?" Quinn asked as he poured coffee into four mismatched mugs and placed a carton of milk beside them.

"After I calmed her down a bit," Garth said, "we went over to your place, Steadman. We saw your car sitting flat in the driveway with four flabby tires—"

"And no one answered our repeated jabs at the doorbell," Lily added. "Then suddenly we heard the roar of a Harley and I knew. I just knew it had to be you, going somewhere and finding another way."

"So we followed you here and when we peeked through the window and saw Quinn holding a gun on you…"

"We broke in," Lily finished.

"I'm glad you did," Quinn said. "But what do we do now?"

Garth leaned forward. "I have a good buddy in the press, with connections to reputable people in the state leadership. With the evidence we've been able to dig up and the testimony Quinn can provide, along with whatever's on that chip Sarah saved for us, I figure we've got a decent shot."

"If we can deliver our cache of proof into the hands of those outside Holloway's corrupt circle, they can break this thing wide open," Steadman said. "We can bring charges and make them stick."

"And prove the charges against Frost were engineered," Lily added. "Getting them dropped."

Steadman bit down on a smile. Frost may be in Lily's doghouse for the moment, but he was glad to see she was committed to getting him out of the jailhouse.

"And we can get justice for Sarah," Quinn said quietly.

"Amen." Steadman held up his mug and the others raised theirs, clinking them gently together.

Garth called his journalist friend and arranged a midnight meeting. None of them wanted to wait until morning with the plan and the evidence burning a hole in their pockets. Every second weighed heavy.

Shortly after eleven, they left the house and Steadman waited with Quinn while he locked the front door.

"Don't know why I bother," Quinn said. "Not when anyone can just waltz in through the back door."

"We'll get it fixed tomorrow," Steadman assured him.

They'd agreed to take Garth's car to the rendezvous and as Steadman turned to join the others walking toward where it was parked on the street, four figures emerged from the shadows. Steadman shouted a warning, but it was too late.

Corvette man had Lily in a tight grasp. Steadman caught the glint of the streetlight on steel as he moved the knife to her throat.

Holloway himself stood beside them. He raised the gun in his hand, pointing it straight at Steadman's head.

"Someone's been shaking a lot of trees in my jurisdiction," he said.

Steadman nodded. "And digging up dirt."

Holloway's eyes narrowed. "Time to put the shovel away, Chief Steadman."

"Not until I've buried you, Holloway."

The judge gave a short, derisive chuckle. "We'll see which one of us is above ground when the sun comes up tomorrow."

A wave of heat surged through Steadman's gut. "At what point in your career did you come to imagine yourself as judge, jury, and executioner?" he asked. "Were you always rotten or did something happen to veer you off the path of justice?"

Holloway took a step closer, lowering the gun's aim to Steadman's stomach. "You're behaving stupidly, Steadman. Why is that? I have always thought of you as a smart man."

Steadman said nothing.

"All the same, I applaud you," the judge continued. "It sounds like you have a very effective plan all laid out."

"How do you know?" Steadman asked, grateful

that his voice sounded cool despite the hammering of his heart.

Holloway shot him a scornful look.

"You had Sarah's house bugged," Steadman concluded.

The judge didn't bother responding. Instead, he motioned toward the knife at Lily's throat. "Take my word on this, Steadman. It's not going to happen the way you planned."

An eerie smile twisted Holloway's lips as he met Steadman's gaze. "We're going to eliminate all your...evidence. But not here. Too messy, too much DNA left behind."

He nodded to his other accomplices and Steadman recognized two members of the Gibson clan. They checked the four of them for weapons, taking Steadman's pocketknife and the pistol from Garth's ankle holster.

One of them stepped to a dark blue van and slid back a panel in its side to expose an empty space without even a pad on the rusty metal floor.

"We have an alternative venue arranged," Holloway said. He gestured with the gun. "Let's go."

Steadman clenched his fists, digging fingernails into his sweaty palms as he cast around for options and came up empty. Corvette guy let go of Lily and pushed her roughly into the van. She rewarded him with a glare that would flay the skin off a rhino.

Quinn climbed into the van, his face blank, not meeting Steadman's eye or anyone else's. Most likely numb and sinking into despair. Garth's eyes flashed with suppressed rage and Steadman thought his must look the same.

He was steamed.

To come so close. To lose so much. It was beyond bearing.

The door rolled shut with a resounding slam and Steadman rocked as the van jerked forward. They were essentially in a cage. Chain link closed off their compartment from the driver's space and spanned across the back doors, as well. Steadman dreaded to think what the vehicle had been designed for.

A sudden urge to kick and scream, like a child throwing a tantrum, washed over him and he fought to restrain it. No good could come from indulging the impulse and he had to be strong for Quinn and Lily.

It wasn't over yet, and he needed to remember that. They all did.

By rising to his knees, Steadman could peer out the windshield. One of the Gibson brothers drove the van as it followed the sable brown Mercedes carrying Holloway and Mr. Corvette.

As Steadman watched, a black SUV sped out from a side street, cutting abruptly in front of the Mercedes. Gibson slammed on the brakes and the van shuddered, coming to a screeching stop, all four of its passengers thrown forward against the chain link.

Steadman regained his balance in time to see another SUV join the first, forming a roadblock. He turned to look out the back window and saw a third vehicle parked behind them.

They were neatly trapped. S.W.A.T. was emblazoned on the door panels of the SUVs.

Rage gave way to overwhelming relief.

Steadman heard shouting and a lot of hubbub from outside, followed by the sound of someone tinkering with the van's side panel. At last, the door slid open and Frost's face, lit by floodlights, grinned in at them.

"Hey, Chief! It looks like we all got a Get Out of Jail Free card today."

Steadman clapped a hand on his partner's shoulder. "How did *you* get out?" he asked as he scrambled out of the van.

"Come on," Frost said, sidelining the question.

He motioned for them to follow. "We're missing the late show."

At the center of the floodlights, the two Gibson brothers stood glowering, hands cuffed behind their backs. Corvette guy, whose name Steadman still hadn't gathered, slumped beside them, similarly cuffed.

As he stared at the spectacle, Steadman was surprised to see Sheriff Polander enter the circle, prodding a manacled Judge Holloway in front of him.

"You're not the only one with access to modern technology," the sheriff told Holloway, his blue eyes popping, crimson blotches standing out sharper than ever, but with a look of eminent satisfaction spread across his face.

"I've had my suspicions over the years about some of your cases, Holloway, but I didn't seriously believe you could be tied up in something so callous, so brazen as to murder one of my deputies and frame another."

Judge Holloway stood in the spotlight, chin lifted as if posing for a photo. Which indeed he was, as the press was out in force, cameras documenting every moment. He maintained a pleasantly neutral expression and ignored Polander completely.

Unfazed, the sheriff continued, well aware of the public eye. "After speaking with Deputy Frost earlier today, I went over your head, Holloway, and got a court order for tracers and listening devices which my people planted on your people."

Steadman stepped forward and held up the data chip he'd taken from the stuffed rabbit.

"Before she was killed," he announced in a loud, clear voice, "Deputy Sarah Jenkins gathered information and evidence incriminating several corrupt members of our community. I believe that information is contained on this storage device, which I am turning over to the officers in charge of this investigation."

He dropped the chip into an evidence bag held open by the deputy whose responsibility it was to collect evidence at the scene. He watched as the man sealed and labeled the bag, documented by a bank of photographers.

"I'd say we now have a preponderance of evidence," Steadman continued, "supporting the charges against you, Judge Holloway." He paused, raising his fist high as a sign of victory.

"Your reign of terror is over!"

Fragrant smoke rose off the grill as Steadman flipped a row of burgers. The smell of the cooking meat made his mouth water and his stomach growl in pleasant anticipation. Using a pair of tongs, he shifted a dozen chicken thighs and stared across the grass to the tall pines waving gently in the breeze, spangled by sunlight.

This was the kind of day that made him believe western Washington was the most beautiful spot on earth. The kind of day that made all the hard things in life worth the effort.

And there was no denying, they'd all been through some hard things of late.

Smiling, he watched his son-in-law toss a frisbee with Frost while his daughter perched on a bench rubbing a hand across the baby bump that grew bigger each time he saw her.

Quinn and his sister sat at a cedar picnic table, playing Scrabble. A portable play pen beside them held a sleeping infant and a babbling three-year old building a tower from colored blocks.

A cool hand touched his cheek and Steadman turned into Vivi's embrace. She gave him a lingering kiss then pulled back, laughing.

"You've been sampling the goods," she accused. "You taste like barbecue sauce."

"Chef's prerogative."

Leaning her head on his shoulder, she said, "I'm

glad to be back where I belong, Rand. Here, by your side."

"Me too."

After a moment, she added, "I'm so glad Sheriff Polander wasn't a bough on the rotten tree. Despite his foibles, I kind of like your boss."

"Yeah. He's a good guy after all. He believed Frost's story and what's more, he wasn't afraid to do something about it. Gives me hope."

They stood together, neither speaking for some moments. Just gathering strength from each other and feeling the goodness of the day.

At length, Vivi said, "Your burgers are burning. I'll ring the dinner bell."

Within minutes, Steadman's family and friends were gathered and waiting, heads bowed while he said grace.

The prayer ended with a heartfelt and unanimous "Amen."

DIRTY LAUNDRY

LEAH R CUTTER

Zeke would admit that alright, maybe, *perhaps* he should have looked more carefully at the client that Beverly, his business partner, had chosen for the next case at *A to Z Investigations*.

However, Beverly was a lot better at *people* than Zeke was, even on his best day. So he'd trusted her to make the right decision.

Give him a computer system to tickle and he'd have it cooing up at him in just a few minutes.

Or something to that effect.

Because he really, *really* didn't want to be thinking about cooing, or worse, *cuddling*, with this current client.

Though Beverly knew it was Zeke's preference to stay indoors at all times instead of braving the Austin Texas weather, she'd still agreed to meet said client at their vulgar McMansion out in the northern suburbs. Zeke was going to have *words* with Beverly about subjecting him to such horrific conditions.

It hadn't helped that she'd insisted on driving her urban assault vehicle instead of his much more economical Smart Car, something about wanting to actually make it to the meeting instead of sliding off the icy roads and into a ditch.

The drive had been harrowing, of course. Little Miss Offensive-Driving-301-trainer-in-waiting had pushed the speed limit, as well as the *safe* distance between cars that one normally assumed. Particularly on an icy Texas highway.

Zeke was *not* overreacting either. That drive really had shaved several years off his life.

And now, he was having to suffer through this client interview.

Mitzi Meyer, said client, sat on the overstuffed couch across from them. She had dirty blonde hair that came from a bottle, blue eyes that were the result of colored contacts, and triple-D breasts (obviously fake) that looked like overfilled water balloons, sure to pop after being stuffed into that tight western-style shirt of hers. Her voice was breathy and high-pitched, with a giggle that bounced up and down on his nerves like a scratchy record.

The rest of the living room was just as tacky, with generic art prints on the walls, uncomfortable designer furniture all done in chrome and black leather, and beige shag carpet that, while trendy, just wasn't practical with the Texas dirt.

"So you see," Mitzi continued in her breathless style, "my husband and I, agreed to call it quits. Really, I thought that Dicky would have been more upset about it." She sniffed, probably trying to decide what would get her the best reaction out of

Zeke and Beverly, tears or a "brave front." Luckily, she appeared to settle on the latter, sparing them all.

"But now, now I think I know *why* he was so amenable to the divorce!" Mitzi said, finally starting to sound a bit more natural. "According to him, we're broke! I know we have more money than he's claiming we have. We've never been in debt. He must be hiding the money he has somewhere."

Zeke nodded. This was actually a fairly typical case for them, searching for hidden resources during a divorce. He glanced at Beverly, who looked sympathetic, perhaps? She couldn't possibly be believing a word that Mitzi was saying, was she?

It was obvious to Zeke that Mitzi was a gold-digger, seeking a large divorce settlement. She probably already had her next sucker on the line. She wouldn't leave a comfortable (though tacky) situation like this without a new home already in sight.

"I know that this is a difficult time for you," Beverly said soothingly. "We'd love to help you find those hidden assets, wouldn't we, Ezekiel?"

Zeke blinked, surprised.

Normally, Beverly would only use his full name —which he hated—when they were undercover and communicating on comms.

Why had she used it in front of this client? Just to make sure that he was listening?

"Of course," Zeke said, still puzzled but willing to play along. "What sort of business is your husband, ah, Dicky, in?"

Mitzi gave him a grateful smile and arched her back.

What, was he supposed to be paying attention to those watermelons of hers? Were they a distraction? Or did she think he'd help her more willingly if she offered herself to him? That he'd work more diligently on her case?

Those fake boobs didn't do much for him, honestly. He much preferred the petite killing machine sitting next to him, demure in her gauzy long-sleeves and skirt, hiding all those wiry muscles.

"Dicky's the King of Suds! He owns a chain of laundry mats, a couple of dog-washing salons, as well as franchises three of those new eco-wash car washes," Mitzi said proudly.

Zeke nodded. While most of his devices had ad blocking, he occasionally did see a commercial or two. So even he had seen the idiotic proclamations from this "King of Suds," portrayed by an older, overweight white man, frequently from a bathtub overflowing with bubbles while he wore a crown.

Unless this Dicky was an idiot (choice of soon-to-be-ex-wife excluded) he probably was making a lot of money.

"Did he recently take on any of those businesses?" Zeke asked, still alert due to Beverly's not-so-subtle hint that he needed to pay more attention.

"No, he's owned them all for years," Mitzi said. "He even owns the buildings that some of the laundry mats are in."

Curiouser.

"Are there any children involved?" Zeke said, figuring that he should at least know how clear Mitzi's claims were.

"None," Mitzi said. "And I'm glad of it," she declared, looking at them defiantly. "Particularly now, since I see how it's ending. It just wouldn't have been right, me ruining my figure for the likes of him."

Of course Mitzi was more concerned about herself than anyone else. Did any other people even live in her universe?

"All right, let us see what we can find out about your husband's finances and business ventures," Zeke told Mitzi. "If he's hiding something, there's a good chance we'll be able to find it. The question is, do you need courtroom-ready proof? Or will just confronting him be enough?"

Because while Zeke was an expert at computer systems (not just hacking, thank you very much) not all of the avenues he explored were strictly legal.

Better to set client expectations at the start.

Mitzi gave a giggle that sent shivers down his spine.

"Oh, just confronting him will do," she assured them. "Once I know where the money is, I can take it from there."

Beverly cast a long glance at Zeke.

Unfortunately, he wasn't the best at reading people. Even Beverly, though he *did* make an effort to understand her facial expressions.

Was that a warning look?

Possibly.

"Give us what you can in terms of your accounts, and we'll do the rest," Zeke assured her.

"Oh, thank you very much!" Mitzi said, going back to that breathless voice of hers.

Zeke was pretty sure she practiced that voice, probably basing it off recordings of Marilyn Monroe singing, "Happy Birthday, Mr. President."

They finally freed themselves from *that house*, as Zeke was starting to call it in his head. For once, he didn't mind being outside, even though it was freezing out there, walking briskly down the driveway to the street where they'd parked.

Of course, Beverly's car hadn't acquired a parking ticket, even though it had been sitting there past the stupidly short amount of time allotted by the HOA during daylight hours.

Zeke didn't start asking questions until after he was snugly belted in, having verified again that yes, indeed, the passenger seat's airbags would deploy.

"So you want to tell me what all that was about?" he asked. Okay, possibly demanded. What? He was cold. The fancy butt warmers in Beverly's vehicle hadn't gone from tentative to blazing yet.

Mitzi, for all her supposed charms, wasn't really their type of client. Despite her oh-so-calculated innocent expressions, she was probably just as guilty as her husband of some sort of wrong-doing.

Beverly gave him a tight smile. "I'll tell you all about it once we get back to the office," she promised.

Huh. Beverly seemed...tense. Like a panther coiled and ready to spring on some unsuspecting gazelle just wandering by, minding his own business.

Zeke gave a long suffering sigh but didn't pester his partner about the actual business at hand.

Hopefully, he wouldn't end up regretting taking this case more than he already did.

Once in the blessed heat of their office, Zeke immediately checked their security systems, making sure that not only had A) no one broken in but B) that they hadn't spoofed his systems, hiding their devilish deeds.

There weren't many who could break through Zeke's own systems, but it always paid to be diligent.

Particularly since the bad guys always recognized that *he* was the brains of the operation, and were much more likely to kidnap him and hold him hostage, rather than Beverly.

Not that he was some damsel in distress who needed rescuing.

At least not today.

But the office was undisturbed, two desks pushed against each other in the middle of the space, his covered with computer gear, hers covered in archaic papers, folders, even books. (And no matter how much he tried *explaining* that all that paper was creating more dust that was likely to give him a sneezing fit, she refused to change her ways. Even went so far as to suggest that he upgrade the fancy air cleaner sitting in the corner that did a marvelous job of keeping all the allergens out of the air.)

Beverly waited to explain until after Zeke had

poured himself more coffee with three creams, no sugar. (He didn't care for sweet things, which was one of the reasons why he wasn't a blob, even with his perpetual distaste of anything resembling physical labor).

Once he was safely ensconced in his marvel of a desk chair that actually *supported* the curvature of his back instead of forcing him to sit in an unnatural position, he gestured for Beverly that he was ready.

"Before I met you, I was working for, well, let's just say one of those three-letter government agencies," Beverly said.

Zeke nodded. He knew that. Those idiots had let her go. Retired her before she was ready to leave. Left her broken and feeling like a failure before he'd stepped in and invited her to work in his newly-minted private investigation firm.

Though that might sound as though he'd saved her, he was well aware of the fact that she had saved him. And continued to rescue him regularly from those all-too-inconvenient kidnappings.

"I wasn't able to close all the cases I'd worked on before I was forced into retirement," Beverly continued, grimacing.

Zeke nodded warily. He'd never gotten all the

details of her previous employment, and hadn't gone digging too deeply, either.

For once, he'd understood that some things were private, and that Beverly would tell him when she was good and ready to.

"Dicky, also known as Richard Meyer, was under investigation by my team for money laundering," Beverly said. "I...I probably shouldn't be telling you this. But I always wanted a chance to put that smarmy bastard away."

Huh. Zeke had *not* been expecting that at all.

"Is that was why you agreed to help Mitzi?" Zeke asked. "Not because you felt sorry for her or something?"

Did he deserve that much of an eyeroll?

No, he did not, thank you very much.

"Mitzi is Dicky's third wife," Beverly told him. "And believe me, they were all just as ditzy. Though I suspect that Mitzi may have a little bit of brain behind those vacuous blue eyes."

Zeke nodded, a little surprised by Beverly's obviously disapproving tone. "I don't know. They might have sucked most of that gray matter out to blow up that chest of hers."

That got him a giggle, Beverly wrinkling her cute, petite nose at him.

"Mitzi is a piece of work," Beverly agreed.

"She probably puts little hearts instead of dots over the I's of her name," Zeke groused, getting another approving smile.

"So, while I know Mitzi doesn't care if we get anything courtroom legal on Dicky, if we can find something that I could anonymously turn into my old office, I'd appreciate it," Beverly said all in a rush.

Zeke wasn't great at reading people. Or a room. But he thought he might have an inkling of what Beverly was feeling.

"You don't need to prove yourself to those assholes," he said quietly. "I know you're absolutely amazing at everything you do. You don't need their approval."

Enough therapy—and, okay, maybe some daytime TV talk shows—had shown him that.

"Thank you," Beverly said, her smile sincere though possibly a bit wobbly. "I know you think so."

"The implication being that you have me snowed over, as effectively as Mitzi has Dicky?" Zeke said. Then he actually put his hands over his mouth, unable to believe that he'd actually said that to Beverly.

He shouldn't confront her. Not ever. Not if he wanted to stay in one conveniently lanky piece and not broken, folded into a pretzel, and stuffed into a dumpster. Before she walked out of his life forever.

"No," Beverly said slowly, as if trying to convince herself.

Zeke sighed and shook his head.

Beverly was amazing. So amazing, in fact, that at some point, someone else would realize it and she'd disappear, leaving him and his detective agency, heading for greener pastures somewhere.

"You are absolutely incredible at what you do," Zeke assured her. "I'm lucky to have you working with me. I know that at some point, you'll get a better offer and leave. Until then, trust me when I tell you that you're great."

His pep talk appeared to have at least made Beverly stop and think for a moment. She tilted her cute head to one side and gazed at him, pensively.

"I wouldn't leave," she assured him. "Not after what you've done for me. I'm not fickle in my loyalties, unlike some people."

"That's good to know," Zeke said, trying to sound sincere but knowing that she'd just lied to him. She would leave him, eventually.

Beverly just shook her head before she continued.

"When Richard Meyer was with wife number

one, Dolores, we were able to gather a lot of evidence. Unfortunately, it wasn't enough to take to a grand jury. We were just about to gather some really important bits, given to us by Dolores. Then, Dolores and Richard reached a settlement. We couldn't close the case without Dolores and that extra evidence she'd been promising us. She started threatening to turn against us, claim that we'd harassed her and led her on, lying under oath about her involvement."

Zeke nodded, already coming up with ideas of places where he could go searching through Dicky's businesses.

"Wife number two, Edina, had signed a better pre-nup than Dolores. We couldn't have talked with her even if she'd wanted to. She had no clue about what Richard was up to, and was content with the money he'd sent her home with," Beverly said.

"Does it make sense for us to try to go and talk with either of these women?" Zeke asked. "And by us, I mean you, of course." While he was always involved in the first interview with a client, after that, they were Beverly's problem.

He just didn't *people* well enough for that to be a good idea.

"I doubt Dolores will talk with me," Beverly

said. "She probably remembers me from the first go around."

"Are you saying that *I* have to go talk with her?" Zeke said, already horrified.

Beverly gave him a teasing smile. "Well...no. I doubt she's changed her mind."

Zeke gave a heartfelt sigh of relief.

"Edina moved back to Mexico, and I doubt that she wants to talk with us either," Beverly said.

"So what's the plan?" Zeke said.

"You go through all the bank accounts and statements that Mitzi provided," Beverly said. "I'm going to go talk with one of my old colleagues, see if they have any ideas, or new information."

Zeke's treacherous mouth spoke without him thinking about it. "But you'll be back, right?"

The brilliant smile Beverly gave him was as warm as Austin summer sunshine. "Of course. I'm not going anywhere."

They gazed at each other for a few moments, as if testing the truth of the statements they'd just made.

"Except, you know, to go talk with one of my old co-workers," Beverly said eventually.

"Go," Zeke said, turning to his computer, his trusty friend, the one who wouldn't leave him. "I'll do my thing in the meanwhile."

"I'll always come back for you," Beverly said softly as she opened the door, not turning back to look at him.

Then she left before he could comment.

As much as Zeke would like to think that Beverly wouldn't leave, that she meant what she said, he knew that the future might contain other things for her. Tasks beyond him and their agency.

There wasn't anything he could do about that now, though.

Instead, he delved into the online world, seeking out Dicky's secrets and dirty laundry.

Zeke was *not* stymied. He was just taking a well-deserved break while he thought about the problem.

All right, so he was going to have to admit to being guilty of assuming incompetence concerning Beverly's former workers. They had let her go, after all, which honestly was a criminal offense, at least as far as he was concerned.

He'd also assumed that the money coming into the laundromat had to be where the illegal money was flowing into the system. That was where the dirty cash came in, right?

However, he hadn't been to a laundromat for over a decade, since college. (And no, he was *not* getting old, despite being thirty-two, now. Besides, Beverly was always going to be older, having just turned thirty-four.)

Laundromats had changed. Instead of saving up quarters, or going to the bank for change, the payments were automated. Everything was done on an app via credit cards.

That meant that payments in and out of the system were able to be tracked much more closely. It would be very difficult for Dicky to claim that he had extra money coming in when he was no longer dealing with cash.

The dog spas and the car washes were much the same: all transactions done via easily trackable monetary avenues.

So where was the dirty money coming in? How was he cleaning it? And where were his substantial profits actually going?

The illegal cash wasn't coming from the rents Richard was collecting. He did own two of the four buildings that housed King of Suds' laundromats. However, as far as Zeke could tell, the other tenants in those places were legitimate businesses and not cheating too much on their taxes. They weren't paying extraordinary amounts of leasing fees that would "hide" some of the money coming in, either.

Dicky *did* have quite a shell game going, with one company acting as a holding company for another, then another on top of that, and another. The sheer number of them was probably what had caught the eye of Beverly's former employer. Zeke hadn't managed to trace the stacked shells to the end of the rainbow, at least not yet.

His gut told him, though, that was yet another dead end.

Was Dicky smart enough to create a variety of shell companies just to give the three-letter agencies something to focus on? Like a magician distracting the public with one hand while the other hand did all the dirty work?

That was possible.

Yet again, Dicky had also married Mitzi, so he couldn't be that much of a financial genius. Mitzi, who'd gladly provided them with legitimate access to all her bank accounts. As well as all of Dicky's, too.

Just as Zeke was about to dive back into his online world, to see if maybe he could find all of Dicky's companies, Beverly came back in from her meeting.

"Hey!" she said, smiling as she walked into the office.

The cold and wind outside had reddened her cheeks, giving her a cute blush.

"Hey, yourself," Zeke said.

He knew that the temperature controls for the room (that he'd installed himself, instead of relying on the generic crap provided by their landlord) hadn't just turned up the heat.

It was still slightly warmer now than it had been.

Must be Beverly's sunny smile.

"You taking a break?" Beverly asked.

Zeke beamed at her. It had taken a little bit of time, but she'd finally learned to ask what he was doing instead of barging in and disturbing him when he might be having really deep thoughts. Even if it looked as though he was just sitting there, staring at nothing.

"I am," Zeke said, pushing back from his desk. "How about you? How was your meeting?"

On the other hand, Zeke had finally gotten used to the give and take of conversation, instead of leaping in and geeking out all over the place about his success (or distinct lack there of, at this point).

"I met with Edmund for coffee," Beverly said.

"Is that his real name?" Zeke couldn't help but asking.

Beverly gave him another grin. "It is. He's very British."

Zeke tried not to imagine a tall, dark, handsome British man bringing such a smile to Beverly's face, but failed utterly.

"According to Edmund, the agency is no longer working on Richard Meyer or his money laundering. Get this—it isn't even considered a cold case, but has been closed and pushed to the side, by order of my former asshole boss," Beverly said, still seemingly full of cheer.

"And that's a good thing?" Zeke asked.

"It is," Beverly said. She leaned closer to Zeke. "It isn't standard operational procedure *at all*," she continued. "Normally, that kind of case would still be considered open. Just because we'd never found enough evidence doesn't mean that someone wouldn't be taking a look at it on an annual basis. So it isn't normal that, uhm, John closed it."

Zeke noticed Beverly's hesitation about mentioning her former boss's name. Was John a fake name? Did she not want to tell Zeke his real name, in case Zeke acted out some of his more vengeful fantasies?

But he didn't bring it up. Instead, he asked, "So

what happened? Did they clear Richard?" Were they actually barking up the wrong tree? Had Richard gone legitimate?

"The reason that my boss gave for closing the case is because all his laundry facilities are now automated," Beverly said. "Richard shut down all the coin operated machines and went to cards and apps."

"That's what I discovered!" Zeke said. "There isn't an obvious way for the money to be placed."

Beverly was still grinning at him, though she wasn't saying anything. Yet.

"And?" Zeke said, prompting her. "Where is the money coming from?"

Beverly pressed her lips together and paused, letting the tension build. "Edmund thinks it's still coming from the laundromats. And I agree."

"Really? How? Where?" Zeke asked.

"I have an idea," Beverly said. "It will involve actually going to one of the locations, though. You got any dirty clothes piled up that we could use?"

And that was how Zeke ended up outside of the northernmost King of Suds laundromat the next morning, waiting in Beverly's warm car, as a line formed up outside the door.

The people in line were all men. All muscular. They looked the type to either have sweaty gym clothes in their over-stuffed duffle bags, or cheap suits that needed the blood cleaned off.

"Who are all these people, and why are they standing in line?" Zeke had to ask after trying to out-stubborn Beverly.

It was far too early in the morning for him. Who did laundry at 7 AM? He generally was lucky to make it to the office before noon. Just before noon, like maybe 11:58. Because if he came in after 12 PM, Beverly would be gone for the rest of the day and he'd be alone.

"I think these people are all supposed to be legitimate business men," Beverly said. "I don't recognize any of them. But it wouldn't surprise me if more than one of them had their own tag-team of three-letter-agency watchers."

"And they follow a regular routine, coming here to drop off their laundry for the week?" Zeke said.

"They do," Beverly said. "Now, I'm sure that some of them are actually legitimate. But the King of Suds has a 'happy hour' when it comes to dropping off your laundry and having other people do it for you. For the first thirty minutes of business every day, you get five dollars off. Or something like that."

"So it's a well-known service," Zeke said, still trying to put the pieces together.

"Yes," Beverly said. "And that's how he justifies the amount of *cash* coming into the store."

"Wait, did you just say cash?" Zeke asked, perking up. At least growing more vaguely alert. There was too much blood in his caffeine system at the moment.

"Yup. That's part of the bargain," Beverly said, grinning just too cheerily this early. "If you pay in cash you get an extra five percent off your load."

"So Dicky's sneaking the cash in right under the noses of the agencies," Zeke mused.

"That's what Edmund thinks," Beverly said. "And, uhm, John did warn him to stay from the case."

Zeke was impressed by how rapidly he put two and two together and came up with ten, particularly given the time of day.

"Is Edmund thinking that perhaps *John* has been wrongfully influenced by Dicky?" Zeke said.

Beverly shrugged. "He didn't say anything like that. And I'm afraid that I don't have good judgment about it, because of what that asshole did to me. But it kinda sorta looks that way."

"Got it," Zeke said. He gave a sigh that sounded impressively emo, even to his jaded ears. "The door's unlocked," he said.

"Go! Get in line!" Beverly said, shooing him from the car.

Zeke unhappily stepped out from the blessed heat and into the freezing cold air. Honestly, his toes were already frozen just from the short walk across the parking lot. That wind was rough enough to peel the skin from his cheeks. Even his eyes hurt, the liquid in them probably freezing.

All right, so maybe not. It was only forty-eight degrees outside.

Horrifyingly cold for a Texas boy.

He joined the end of the line of equally grumpy men. No one looked at him. They all were very careful not to look at anyone else in line.

If this had been a line for a bathroom, he'd see the point.

Here? In this weather? There should be at least a little chatter. Some sort of reference to the hell they were currently standing in.

Zeke didn't feel inclined to start any conversation himself—talking to people was never going to be natural for him. But he'd studied situations like this. Created a manual of sorts for himself, so he'd know how to fit in.

It was odd.

Half a dozen other men joined the line behind

him, all silently shuffling forward into the blessed heat of the building.

However, the moment Zeke stepped inside, he regretted it.

Of course, they used scented laundry soap as well as fabric softener here. His eyes started watering immediately. Though he knew it wasn't possible, he still felt hives already starting to break out all across his sensitive skin.

He suffered in silence, though, as the line moved forward.

The woman behind the desk looked like a mafia grandmother, her white face heavily wrinkled, gray hair pulled up into a neat bun, dark eyes that could cut you to shreds, and probably packing an automated sub-machine gun in her voluminous chest.

In most small businesses, customer service was key. Regulars—and Zeke understood from Beverly that all of these men came here weekly—should be greeted by name, their preferences already known.

But Scary Grandma up there barely glanced at any of her customers. They emptied out their clothes into the waiting basket, ready to be weighed. Once that number was written down, they received a receipt and walked away, out the door with their empty bag, looking relieved, maybe?

Except that none of them were getting out their wallets. Would they not pay until they came back and picked up their clothes? Was that normal?

When it was Zeke's turn, he followed along with the script, putting his clothes into the basket to be weighed. Then he said, "No scented detergents."

Really, he didn't want to have to replace all the clothes he'd brought in. Or wash them a dozen times in vinegar to remove the smell.

That earned him a piercing look from the old woman.

"Nothing smelly," she said, her tone indicating that Zeke, himself, was already smelly enough.

"Thank you," Zeke said. He took the slip of paper from her. "When will the clothes be ready?"

Instead of replying, or even looking at him again, she tapped her pen on the sign next to her.

All laundry brought in to be washed before 7:30 AM would be ready after 2 PM. No additional loads would be accepted after 11 AM.

"Thank you," Zeke said again as he hurried out the door and back to the sanctuary of Beverly's car.

"I don't know if this is a real lead or not," Zeke warned as he strapped himself in before Beverly could take off and assault something else with her vehicle.

She shrugged. "We'll come back this afternoon and see." She paused, then added, "Want to go out for breakfast? There's a restaurant near here that has an excellent food safety score. I checked."

"Do they have good coffee?" Zeke asked warily. At this point in the morning it might be far too early for him to be diluting his caffeine system with food.

"I don't know," Beverly said, sounding disappointed.

"Let's go see, then," Zeke said, telling himself that the high rating—and spending more time outside the office with Beverly—was much more important than great coffee. Good enough would be good enough for now. The taste didn't matter as much as the caffeine.

Beverly grinned at him, and Zeke knew that he'd made the right choice.

Anything to keep her smiling that way.

When Zeke went to pick up his laundry later that afternoon, a young blonde woman with a thick Russian accent was working behind the counter. She wore a tight T-shirt and had perky tits as fake as Mitzi's.

Maybe Mafia Grandma was making soup. Or cookies. Or some other concoction that would hide whatever poison she was using that day.

The woman barely glanced at his receipt before she quoted him an outrageous price.

Eighty dollars just for a single load of laundry? When he hadn't even asked for pressed shirts, starch, or anything else?

"Are you sure?" Zeke said. No, his voice didn't squeal as he said that. Much.

That got the woman to look up at him, then at the ticket.

"Oh. Sorry. No, for you..." she paused, then reached for a calculator to figure out his total.

It was closer to twenty dollars, what with the five dollars off for coming in early as well as the discount for cash.

Zeke paid, asking for a receipt (it was a business expense, after all) then carried the neatly folded pile back to Beverly's car.

He was still going to have to wash it himself. A couple of times. Though they hadn't used smelly detergent, his clothes had still picked up some of the scent just by proximity. That, too, was going to be a business expense.

"Yup. The cash is coming in through the

laundry business," Zeke said, retelling his events to his partner.

Beverly nodded, looking vindicated. "Good. Now, you just have to do your magic and figure out where it's going."

It took Zeke most of the week to track down Dicky's sprawling empire, now that he had a clue where at least some of the dirty cash was coming from.

As he'd suspected, the shell companies were just a way to keep someone tied up in knots and not actually paying attention to what was going on right in front of their noses.

Namely, the actual properties that Dicky owned.

Property was a great way to hide cash. Particularly property that was used by some of those illegitimate businessmen, who would pay rent with dirty money.

At first glance, they'd all seemed legal. Passed a quick sniff test.

On digging further, though…seemed that more than one of the other businesses renting from Dicky paid their rent in cash. No money was going out from their accounts. However, large amounts were being regularly deposited by Dicky, then transferred automatically into another shadowy corporation that paid dividends to people who owned stock in the company.

And those people just happened to be the same individuals renting from Dicky.

The government couldn't prove the connection. But to Zeke, it was obvious.

Dicky had two sources of questionable income: one from the cash coming into the laundromats, and the other from the rents. (Though the dog salons and the car washes also had "happy hours" for people who paid in cash, as far as Beverly could tell, no one was paying extraordinary amounts.)

Mitzi was right to question Dicky's wealth. A lot of money was coming in. Only some of it, though, was going back out.

Finding the sources of money coming into the laundering machine was only half the equation. The other half was finding the hidden assets.

It wasn't until Zeke got into Dicky's first wife's —Dolores Meyer's—accounts that he figured out the truth. Dicky was paying her a lot of alimony. Like six figures worth. But Dolores didn't have that much money remaining in her accounts by the end of each month.

She was taking out large cash payments on a regular basis.

It was yet another way that Dicky was cleaning

the money: paying it out to Dolores, who returned it to him in cash.

Zeke presented his findings to Beverly at the end of the week, walking her through all the trails of cash that he'd found.

Beverly grinned at him at the end of it, praising him for the color coding he'd done to make the graphs easier to read.

"But now what do we do?" Zeke asked. "Do we send this all to Mitzi? To your former employer? Both? Neither?"

He really wasn't sure what Beverly would want to do. He had the feeling that she'd really like to take down her former boss, the one who'd claimed that there was nothing left to investigate in terms of Richard Meyer.

"We do have a duty to our client," Beverly said slowly.

"But you're afraid that if we show her this, she'll get a payoff like Dolores, and won't talk anymore?" Zeke guessed.

"Yes," Beverly agreed. "And if I give it to, uhm, John, my former boss, the information might just disappear as well."

"Can you work with Edmund?" Zeke said, though he hated having to suggest it. They really had moved beyond their usual payrate by uncovering such a large organization.

And if they weren't careful, well, Zeke would probably get kidnapped again.

Or worse.

Beverly nodded. "I'll go talk with him again."

Zeke gave her a thumbnail drive with all the information on it, then arranged for the pair of them to meet for coffee after her meeting with Edmund.

In part, because he wanted to make sure that Edmund didn't try anything. Not that Zeke would be any good at a rescue. However, he might be able to think of something creative, particularly if it were Beverly's neck on the line.

But also because it was better to spend time with her. He'd discovered that though he still didn't like people, in general, he did enjoy being with Beverly, both in and out of the office.

Besides, he needed to save up all the memories he could.

Before she left him.

After the meeting with Edmund (which went on for far too long for Zeke's fragile system), Beverly agreed to wait another two days before presenting their findings to Mitzi. That meeting was as uncomfortable as the first. At least Mitzi hadn't balked at paying their bill up front, though Zeke had the feeling that if Beverly hadn't been there, she might have offered "services" to him in lieu of payment.

Which, quite frankly, ewww.

It was two weeks later, when they were solidly in the middle of the next case, before Edmund sent a text to Beverly, asking for her to meet with him again, ending the message with a simple smile emoji.

Though Zeke offered to go with, Beverly declined.

Zeke took that as the beginning of the end.

Edmund would offer Beverly her old position. Which Beverly would take. Maybe not immediately, but eventually.

Zeke wasn't sure what he'd do once he lost her. *A to Z Investigations* might be finished at that point.

So he waited impatiently at the office, supposedly digging into their current case but honestly, just cruising around the dark web, seeing what sort of trouble he'd get himself into if he actually went ahead and found someone to take care of Beverly's old boss (whose name was *not* John, but Zeke continued to play dumb regarding that).

Beverly came in all smiles, her cute nose almost wrinkled in delight.

Zeke sighed internally and prepared for the worst.

He waited (mostly) patiently as Beverly made herself a cup of peppermint tea (whoever told her that she needed less caffeine in her life was seriously on his "find them and mess them up for good" list). Only when she'd finally sat at her desk did he pounce.

"So what happened? What did Edmund say? Is Dicky going away for good? Do I need to start hiding our own assets? Are we safe? Or do we have to think about going into hiding as well?"

All right, so maybe, perhaps, he'd had enough caffeine that afternoon to fuel an all-nighter being pulled by idiotic college football players, hoping to score well on their next chemistry exam. (Not that he had *any* sort of experience helping that particular brand of moron out. No, really. He'd made all his college funds in legitimate ways. Not by shaking down the neanderthals who used to bully him in high school.)

Beverly just grinned at him, taking a deliberate sip of her tea, making him wait more.

"I think we're in the clear," she said eventually, not teasing him more. "The agency is going to 'fix' the problem. Arrest warrants have already been signed and executed. Richard Meyer is now a problem of the federal judiciary system."

"And we trust that they'll get it right?" Zeke asked cautiously.

"We do. Particularly since it appears that *John* has left the country and appears to have landed in a country that doesn't have extradition agreements with the US," she said. She actually sounded aggrieved at that.

"So you got your old boss," Zeke said, determined to be happy for her.

"I did," Beverly said smugly. "And yes, it feels good. Even though he isn't facing justice, at least he's no longer in charge."

Zeke swallowed hard at that. He sighed. "And when are you going back?"

"Back?" Beverly said. She sounded puzzled but there was a twinkle in her eye that Zeke knew meant that she was teasing him.

"Back to your old job?" Zeke said. "Back to Edmund?"

He kept imagining a tall, debonair British man with impeccable manners and a flair for the exotic wining and dining Beverly.

Beverly chuckled and shook her head.

"There is no going back," she said seriously. "Only forward. I like being my own boss," she added. "Not answering to some government agency. Here, I know I can do some good. There, well, sometimes the jobs were a little more gray than I was comfortable with."

"Huh," Zeke said. It had never occurred to him that straight-forward Beverly, who always wanted to play by the rules, might have not been as much in her past.

Then again, that might be *why* she was so insistent on it now.

"And Edmund? Surely he wants you back?" Zeke said.

"He did ask whether I was interested," Beverly admitted. "But," she said, holding up her hand before Zeke could pounce and say something more, "I also told him no. And made him understand that not only was I not coming back, I wouldn't appreciate any pressure from him or anyone else in the matter."

"Really?" Zeke asked, surprised. She really didn't want to go back that badly?

"I believe the phrase, 'I know where you live,' might have been used," Beverly admitted seriously. "Not that I would ever harm a hair on his head. Or his husband's."

"What? Huh?" Zeke said, totally thrown for a loop.

"Edmund has a lovely husband. Ethan," Beverly said. "I wouldn't ever threaten Ethan. While Edmund has official training in various martial arts, Ethan, well, he's chaos incarnate. I pity anyone who targets Edmund while Ethan's around."

"I see," Zeke said, though he didn't.

"You're not getting rid of me that easily," Beverly said, turning serious on him.

Zeke sat for a moment, letting her statement sink in.

She wasn't going anywhere. Not for now, possibly not ever, though that was too long of a period of time to think about.

"You're not getting rid of me either," Zeke breathed out, unable to stop himself from affirming his commitment.

"Good," Beverly said softly.

They sat for a moment in the still of the office, a golden time with the sun just peeking through the clouds and lighting the space.

Beverly broke first. "So how is the current case going?"

"Right. Business," Zeke said, nodding. He brought her up to date on the research he'd been doing, and they planned out their next steps. Beverly left to go talk with someone who might be able to help and Zeke was on his own again.

Before he got back to work, Zeke sat there for a while, thinking hard about what Beverly had just said.

She wasn't leaving him, or the agency. Not while there was still some good that she could do without delving too far into the gray. A life to be lived without dirty laundry.

What did that mean for their future? Could Zeke hope? Plan? How long would her loyalty last?

Questions for future Zeke.

Current Zeke turned back to his computer, but instead of trying to solve the most recent case, he went back through his files looking for new cases. A continuous stream of them, so they'd always be busy.

He'd do whatever he must to keep Beverly by his side for a while longer.

RECKLESS ENDANGERMENT

DIANA DEVERELL

The hand-forged iron knocker thumped on Winnie Yates Denver's sturdy six-panel front door. The forceful sound of the hard knock on Douglas fir carried easily to the rear of the one-story brick house she shared with her husband Jake and son Elijah.

Winnie glanced at the bottom right corner of the Lenovo flat screen she relied on in her compact home office. The time was one o'clock on this first Monday afternoon in April. Her bookkeeping client Phil Johnson had arrived on schedule.

Phil had spent his morning at the restaurant he owned ten miles east of her Spokane Valley home. Being precisely on time meant he'd prioritized their appointment over his end-of-shift tasks at Valley Pub and Grill.

And a damn good thing he had. This meeting was also Winnie's top priority. Phil had a problem and if he solved it the wrong way, *she'd* have a bigger problem.

Rolling her office chair back from the desk, Winnie got to her feet, and stepped out into the slate-floored hallway leading to the entry. Sunshine poured from the two skylights above the hallway, telling her that this morning's cloud cover had lifted.

Better weather was a good omen and Winnie let

herself hope. Phil was a good guy and he was happy with her work. But she knew he'd resist taking her advice. Though, if she handled him carefully, she might be able to persuade him to go along with her.

Stepping forward, she spotted the top of Phil's shaved head through the center glass panel of the three windows topping her front door. She'd trained originally as a stylist and she automatically registered that his skull was nicely shaped and the no-hair look still suited him.

Moving quickly on her black rubber-soled flats, she reached the entry foyer and paused to smooth the wrinkles from her long-sleeved wine-colored silk T-shirt. She also brushed eraser crumbs off her black jeans. Her business-casual outfit was appropriate for a competent self-employed bookkeeper working efficiently from her home.

Winnie gently patted her dark-chocolate bob, reassuring herself that every strand was still in place. On Saturday, her colorist had subtly brightened the near-black shade by applying babylights to the gray strands that were becoming more abundant now she'd reached age forty-eight. The ultra-fine, thin highlights mimicked the way hair naturally lightens after a summer spent in the sun.

The early tan she'd gotten on her cheeks while watching nine-year-old Elijah play spring soccer went well with the lighter hair color. The new do made her feel like a woman who had her act together. Which was how she needed Phil to see her for the next hour.

Winnie pulled the door open and breathed in a springy grass-scented breeze. She also got a hint of citrus, likely from Phil's aftershave.

He wore an oversize car coat in the pale shade of brown called desert. The left corner of the semi-spread collar was casually flipped up, creating a dashing effect. She spotted a tiny Tommy Hilfiger black, white, and red flag on the coat's cuff.

Phil always seemed to be well-groomed and well-dressed when he was out in public. Appearances mattered to him. Winnie had done everything she could to give off a similar self-confident vibe.

Waving him indoors, Winnie inclined her head to the five iron hooks mounted on the wall. "Hang up your coat and follow me to the kitchen," she said. "My little office isn't furnished for client meetings. We'll be more comfortable sitting at the kitchen table while I tell you what I found."

"Fine with me." Giving her a questioning look, Phil added, "I assume only the two of us are present today."

"Of course," Winnie replied. "I don't pick

Elijah up from soccer practice until three-thirty and Jake won't be home before five."

"Is Jake still working at Lost Horse Distillery?" Phil asked.

Winnie laughed. "Last week, he hit the ten-year mark with them. The business has grown a lot since he started and he's their operations manager now."

"They certainly hand-craft a fine wheat bourbon," Phil said. "Very popular with our customers."

He pulled off his coat, giving her a flash of a larger Tommy Hilfiger flag on the inside of the collar at the back. Beneath the coat, he wore a long-sleeved white shirt tucked into dark-brown corduroy trousers.

Winnie heard the click of Phil's oxblood penny loafers on the flooring as she led him down the sunlit hallway to the rear of the house. She got him settled in an armless wooden chair at the round kitchen table, his back to the glass window framing a view of the distant mountain range.

When he declined her offer to make coffee, Winnie claimed the chair across from him.

Phil gestured at the immaculate room. "You and your family have a lovely home in a beautiful setting."

His smile colored his tone and Winnie beamed

back at him. "Thanks. We're very happy in this house. I appreciate your willingness to meet at my home instead of having me come to The Valley Pub and Grill. I don't want any of your employees to overhear what I have to tell you."

"Me, neither." Phil sighed. "I don't want to alarm them while we figure this out. I told no one I'm meeting with you."

Winnie echoed his sigh. "I'm afraid I don't have good news. After our phone conversation yesterday, I dug into the expense and income records for your place over the past six months. My results agree with the opinion you gave me."

Phil shrugged. "Thanks for checking. Given how busy we've been, my gut tells me the net profit is lower than it should be. I was hoping you'd find I was mistaken."

"I'm sorry, but no such luck," Winnie replied. "Your gut was correct."

"Tell me what figures you came up with," Phil said.

"The software you're using to track expenditures made it easy for me to total the precise amounts of your key supplies that you bought during the past six months," Winnie began. "I compared those figures to the amounts you bought during the same period last year. You increased the quantity of supplies purchased by roughly twenty percent. The actual costs increased by another couple of percentage points because prices also rose."

Phil shook his head. "I raised my prices to cover the increase in costs. And yet my gross revenue from food sales stagnated. We're heading into the summer tourist season, which is usually when my traffic is highest. I need to hire temporary staff to deal with the bigger crowds. But I won't do that until I figure out why revenue hasn't gone up."

"I thought over what may be going wrong and I have a tentative plan to run by you." Winnie leaned forward. "You recall I got my start as a bookkeeper working for LaNoir Kennedy."

Phil nodded. "LaNoir's been taking care of my wife's hair and nails for the past twenty years. When I decided in 2020 to stop keeping my own books and contract for the service, LaNoir recommended you. Told me you enrolled in community college to study the subject while you worked up from shampoo girl to hair stylist to bookkeeper assistant. You took over her books fulltime in 2016 and have been with her as she expanded to her current four salons."

"Nice recap of my career change," Winnie said.

"But the point I want to make is that my experience with LaNoir may be relevant to your problem."

Phil raised an eyebrow. "How so?"

"For me as a bookkeeper, a beauty salon and a restaurant have important characteristics in common. Both you and LaNoir employ more than a dozen people who sell products and services on your premises to a range of customers. In fact, LaNoir had a similar financial disparity last year in one of her salons. We decided to begin by investigating two of the most probable explanations."

Winnie raised her right hand, fingers spread, and used the pointer finger on her left hand to tick them off. "First, someone was stealing supplies. Or, second, someone was stealing from payments made in cash rather than by credit card."

"Maybe a thief can commit those crimes in a salon without anyone noticing," Phil said. "But not at The Valley Pub and Grill. Either I'm in the building or Tara is. One of us would spot outright theft."

Winnie hadn't yet met Tara but the name was in her files. Clarifying, she said, "You hired Tara North when your former manager retired six months ago?"

"Yes," Phil confirmed. "When my long-time manager left in October, I hired Tara North. She works from noon to eight, Friday through Tuesday. I cover the morning shift every day, plus noon to eight on Wednesdays and Thursdays. As I said, one of us is always on the premises."

Winnie nodded. "Your revenue decline is significantly higher than what LaNoir experienced. Clearly, greater quantities of supplies and/or cash are being taken by your thief. Neither you nor Tara would fail to see truckloads of food disappearing from your storeroom or bags of currency from your cash drawer."

"My point, exactly," Phil said.

"We found that it was possible for a thief to stay under the radar at LaNoir's. She stole only small quantities of product that could be hidden in an apron pocket. That surreptitious siphoning wasn't obvious but when repeated daily it made enough of a dent in LaNoir's revenue to get her attention."

Phil frowned. "I suppose someone could use a similar technique at my place. If I alert Tara to that possibility of repeated small-scale theft, one or both of us should be able to catch the thief red handed."

Winnie had assumed Phil would involve his manager in the surveillance. For him, Tara was above suspicion. Phil was always eager to think the best of others.

Not Winnie. She'd learned the hard way not to

trust strangers. Whenever she entered into a relationship with someone new, her automatic distrust kicked in.

A relationship as casual as being the bookkeeper for the man who employed Tara North was enough to trigger Winnie's distrust of the woman.

Leaning toward Phil, Winnie delivered the warning she'd prepared in advance. "You want to find out if one of your employees is ripping you off. You have to keep Tara in the dark while you're doing that. You can't let any of your staff know they're being watched. You can't risk Tara revealing your secret scrutiny to someone, either accidentally, or because she thinks that particular employee couldn't be guilty."

Phil's frown deepened. "Tara has years of experience in the restaurant business," he said. "Like many of the best workers in our field, she changes jobs often to expand her skill set. She's up-to-date on the newest restaurant software programs and clear on current best practices. I've drawn on her wealth of knowledge to fine-tune our procedures. She'll be an asset to my investigation."

Damn. Winnie was shocked. In the past five minutes, Phil had rattled off a string of facts as if they proved Tara's value.

Tara took over as manager six months ago.

Tara closes out the till five nights a week.
Tara changes jobs often.
Tara is an expert on restaurant software.

Four red flags flying in Winnie's face and Phil couldn't see them.

Tara was positioned better than anyone else working in the restaurant to steal from Phil. Winnie had to convince Phil to treat Tara the same as his other employees.

Keeping her tone and expression neutral, Winnie said, "Maybe Tara can help after you verify she's trustworthy. But we can't give her or anyone else a free pass in the beginning."

Phil gave a grunt of disagreement. "I pay Tara a hundred thousand dollars a year. She has no reason to steal from me. I see no risk in her helping me right from the start."

"No risk to you, maybe," Winnie said. "But involving Tara this early is an unacceptable risk for me. As your bookkeeper, I will always be the first person law enforcement investigates when you tell them you've found signs someone is embezzling from you. And my personal history will likely mean I'll become their only suspect."

"Whoa." Phil waved his hands in the air. "I haven't said I'm taking my problem to law enforcement."

Winnie sighed. "You may have no choice if you want to find the perpetrator and stop them stealing from you and any future employer. For my own protection, we have to identify the wrongdoer and collect evidence of their guilt *before* we report the crime."

Phil's disbelief was obvious from the expression on his face. Winnie knew he was going to dismiss her advice again.

"You have no reason to worry," he said to her. "Your personal history didn't stop me from hiring you. LaNoir was confident you wouldn't do anything illegal that could land you back in prison. Surely, after nine years without a misstep, your past won't be relevant to law enforcement, either."

Winnie gave a sour laugh. "I served fifteen years in prison for theft and other crimes. No law enforcement officer will ignore that I'm a convicted felon. And none will gloss over the fact that I regularly attend AA meetings because of my drug and alcohol addictions. They won't bother looking for another suspect until they've investigated me thoroughly."

"Of course, I don't want the cops bothering you," Phil said. "But I don't see how I can surveil all my employees on my own. I'll need help. And Tara's best-placed to give me a hand."

"It was also impossible for LaNoir to watch all her stylists," Winnie said. "Maybe you want to try the solution she used."

She slid a business card across the table to Phil. "This is the fellow who installed hidden miniature surveillance cameras in LaNoir's Hair and Nails. With his help, she recorded one of her stylists stealing expensive products, one bottle at a time. LaNoir put the recording in the hands of law enforcement and told them she wanted to press charges for theft."

Phil's eyes widened. "I wouldn't have guessed that soft-hearted LaNoir would get an employee arrested."

"LaNoir is a wonderful person," Winnie said. "She believes in giving people second chances. But she'd caught this employee stealing before. That first time, LaNoir demanded the woman pay for what she'd stolen. The woman paid up and promised she wouldn't steal again. LaNoir let her keep her job. And the woman failed to keep her word."

"I see," said Phil. "I can understand why LaNoir didn't give the woman a third chance."

Winnie drew her chin down in a sharp nod of agreement "The woman pled guilty to the more recent theft, paid a hefty fine, and served ten months in jail. And because LaNoir gave law enforcement evidence that her employee was guilty, they had no reason to expand their investigation to include LaNoir's bookkeeper."

Phil ran a hand over his scalp. "I see why this situation makes you nervous. But I can't imagine you stealing from me."

Winnie sniffed. "Trust me, without a more compelling suspect, local law enforcement will have no difficulty imagining me doing that. Their forensic accountants will comb through all the files of Denver Bookkeeping Services in search of fraud. Maybe LaNoir and you will continue to use my services. But the hint that I might be involved in fraud will damage me with newer clients. I'm sure I'd lose some and replacing them won't be easy."

"I get your point." Phil tapped the card on the table. "Okay. I agree this is the right solution. I won't involve Tara yet. I'll give this a guy a call as soon as I get home. See what he can do for me."

"Thanks," Winnie said. "That lets me breathe a little easier."

Phil pushed back from the table and stood. "And now, I better let you collect your son from soccer practice. I'll give you a call when I have new information."

Winnie walked him to the door, watched him don his coat, and gave him a goodbye handshake.

Closing the front door, Winnie collapsed with her back against it.

Phil was going to handle things the way she wanted. Well, she was ninety percent sure she'd convinced him not to give Tara a chance to cover her tracks. Couldn't be a hundred percent certain because Phil still didn't seem to see his manager as a viable suspect.

Winnie was pretty sure that Tara was the culprit. Still, she knew that fifteen years behind bars had given her a very dark view of humanity. Ninety percent of her fellow inmates looked out only for themselves. Women tried to become friends with Winnie only when she had something they wanted to take away from her.

Her wariness had grown beyond females and felons to include all strangers. When Jake first showed a romantic interest in her, she was sure he had to be a crook. Took her a while to decide he wasn't. She wouldn't tell Jake that she pushed Phil to train his secret cameras on Tara. No need to remind her loving husband of how close she'd come to ruining everything between them.

Winnie lifted her Navy duffel coat off the hook, put it on, and patted the pocket to feel her keys and driver's license inside. Time to pick up Elijah.

They'd come home and she'd make dinner for him and Jake. Keep her perfect little family safe. She wouldn't allow fallout from Tara North's reckless embezzlement to wreck her own wonderful life.

Winnie was at home alone on Saturday afternoon when Phil phoned.

"We put the cameras in place on Wednesday night," he told her. "Captured nothing suspicious on Thursday. But you need to see what we recorded last night after closing. Is this a good time to drop by?"

"Your timing is perfect," Winnie said. "Jake and Elijah just set off on their bikes and won't be back for an hour."

"I'll be right there," Phil replied.

Ten minutes later, she and Phil were in her office, eyes focused on her desktop screen as they watched a video file stored on his thumb drive.

The screen showed Tara North working the restaurant computer. The camera captured both her fingers on the keyboard and the computer screen above it.

Phil paused the recording.

"You're seeing Tara alter the billing records to delete half of the payments made in cash," he explained. "An override that allows management to correct for refunds made to dissatisfied customers and similar anomalies where food was served but not paid for."

Winnie frowned. "When you say management, you mean only you and Tara can do that?"

Phil grunted agreement. "And only Tara knows how to make illegitimate changes appear to be legitimate. Part of the vast experience she gained while ripping off her former employers, I'm sure. You'll enjoy this next bit."

Three minutes later, the tape showed Tara finish altering records and open the cash drawer. She slipped paper currency into her purse.

Phil paused the tape again. "Given the changes she made to the records, I'm guessing she siphoned off at least a hundred dollars last night. Not a lot of money. But if she averaged that amount every night she worked for the last six months, it added up to more than fourteen thousand dollars.

Winnie knew the Washington State laws regarding embezzlement. "Which makes the crime a class B felony," she said. "Punishable by a maximum of ten years in jail and a twenty-thousand-dollar fine."

Phil whistled. "Looks like she's had plenty of practice. I'm surprised nobody caught on to her before."

"Probably why she changed jobs so often," Winnie said. "Left before people were alarmed enough to investigate."

"I paid her a top salary. I still don't understand why she stole from me," Phil said. "Why take the risk?"

"Addiction is something I know first-hand," Winnie said. "The definition that makes most sense to me is that addicted people are driven to do things that are not in their own best interest. I bet Tara gets her buzz from paying herself a big tip with your money. Waitresses love having their pockets full of tip money. I think the buzz is more important than the cash."

"You may be right about her motivation," Phil said. "I won't let her walk away from this job unpunished, like she probably has from every other place she's worked. I will follow LaNoir's example. Press charges against Tara for theft."

"I think you have to do that," Winnie agreed. "You can't let Tara move on to a new victim."

"I have no contacts in the offices of the Spokane

County Prosecutor or Sheriff," Phil said. "Do you think LaNoir can direct me to the right person?"

"Have you heard of the Spokane SIU, the Special Investigations Unit?" Winnie asked.

Phil's forehead wrinkled. "Isn't that unit part of the Washington State Patrol?"

"Yes," Winnie replied. "They based the SIU in Spokane to support local law enforcement in Eastern Washington. They often assist the Spokane County sheriff. LaNoir took her evidence to the SIU, and they worked with the sheriff to make the arrest. I can give you the name of the trooper in charge."

Phil grinned. "And since he knows you through LaNoir, you don't risk getting investigated yourself?"

Winnie chuckled and said, "I'll be fine. Thank you for looking out for me."

Phil laughed. "Thank *you* for looking out for *me*. I'm glad I took your advice."

"Me, too." Winnie grinned. "I'm really glad."

THAT'S NOT MY DADDY—THAT'S AN IMPOSTER!

CHRIS CHAN

"Miss Kaiming, Mr. Funderburke...you have to do something. My stepmother did something to my daddy and replaced him with an imposter!"

Daisy, a six-year-old first-grader, was sitting in one of the big black vinyl chairs in my office. The chair was so big and Daisy was so tiny that it made her look like a little doll. She looked scared, but also defiant.

My girlfriend Nerissa and I shared a glance. This was exactly the sort of thing for which my job as Student Advocate was created for the young people attending the K-12 school Cuthbertson Hall in Milwaukee, Wisconsin. If Daisy had gone to the police, or to the press, the odds that they would've taken Daisy seriously would be miniscule at best. That's why I'm eternally grateful to my alma mater for taking pity on me, a lawyer who couldn't find a job in the legal profession. There's a reason for that —early in my career I got over a dozen formerly respected lawyers and judges disbarred after I proved they were involved in corrupt moneymaking schemes. Since then, instead of being acclaimed as a hero, I've been *persona non grata* in a lot of legal circles, which is why I got into the private detection business. I'm more than O.K. with the turn my career took, especially when I discovered just how many young people feel helpless when they're caught up in situations beyond their control.

I cleared my throat. "Daisy, could you please tell me your story from the beginning?"

She nodded. "You know my daddy, right, Mr. Funderburke?"

"Well, I've heard of him, but we've never met." I turned to Nerissa. "Have you ever been introduced to him?"

Nerissa shook her head. "If a parent doesn't have a kid in the high school, I'm unlikely to have much contact with them."

Neither us wanted to say what we actually knew about Doug Ottovorde. The scion of a wealthy family who had donated tons of money to Cuthbertson Hall over the years and even had a reading room named after them, he'd had quite the reputation for being a playboy for most of his twenties and thirties until he'd finally married, settled down, and had Daisy. Tragically, his first wife got an aggressive form of cancer when Daisy was two and passed away soon afterwards. A year ago, the widower met a woman over twenty years his junior during a business trip. Despite an avalanche of rumors and whispers, no one at Cuthbertson knew for sure just what the second Mrs. Ottovorde had done before their marriage, nor did anybody know the exact circumstances as to how the pair had met. All anybody knew is that before you could say "trophy wife," Doug Ottovorde was remarried to a twenty-four-year-old platinum blonde named Brielle.

"What's your relationship like with your stepmother?" I asked.

Daisy squirmed. "Until today, she's been all right. Not a wicked stepmother, you know, just... not that interested in me. We've mostly stayed out of each other's way the past year."

I nodded. Daisy wasn't alone in her feelings. Doug Ottovorde's mother was a prominent figure in Milwaukee society, and the Ottovorde family matriarch's distaste for her new daughter-in-law was common knowledge amongst the school gossips.

"So, nothing to make you think that she was planning on getting rid of your father and swapping him out with a replacement?"

"No. As far as I could tell, they seemed to be getting along really well. Brielle and I really haven't liked or disliked each other, but I figured if Daddy was happy, I'd live with it."

"So no indication that anything horrible was going to happen?"

"Nope. Not until last night."

Nerissa arched her eyebrows. "What happened then?"

"Well, for the last few days I've been staying at my friend Alexis Lakie's house. Daddy and Brielle have been overseas on a business trip, so they left me with the Lakies for a little while. They were supposed to be back tomorrow. But I was telling Alexis about this new board game I have, and she wanted to play it, so Mrs. Lakie drove us to my house, and I found Brielle there with four other people. As soon as I walked in the house, Brielle started freaking out, and shrieked, 'Daisy! You're not supposed to be here!'"

"Not a very warm welcome," I commented.

"Nope. I explained what I was doing back home, and three of the other people in the room introduced themselves as Daddy's business associates from out of state. They were really friendly, and they explained that they were working with him on an important business deal, and they were working out the details before they signed the final papers."

"Is the business deal the reason why they came back early?" I asked.

"I guess." Then I turned to the fourth stranger in the room and asked him, "And who are you?" He just laughed and said, "Why Daisy, I'm your father.

You know that." Then he looked at the other three people I just met, who looked stunned, and he laughed again and said, 'I just shaved my beard. My own daughter didn't recognize me.'"

I was getting a knot in my stomach, because I sensed that something pretty messed up was happening. "But beard or no beard, you knew this guy wasn't your father?"

"No, he wasn't! He was much younger than Daddy, and his hair was all brown—it didn't have any gray in it. He looked kind of like Daddy, and his voice was a lot like Daddy's, but it wasn't him. Before I could say anything, Brielle hustled me out of the living room, and started whispering to Mrs. Lakie that it would be great if they could let me stay with them for another couple of days. Mrs. Lakie agreed, and Brielle hustled us out of the house, and told us that she was sorry, but the investors demanded total privacy, and we needed to leave them alone while they worked out sensitive business details."

"Did you get your board game?" I asked.

"Yes. I'd forgotten all about it, but Alexis asked about the game right after Brielle pushed us out the door, so Brielle just groaned, said 'Wait a sec,' and closed the door on us. She reopened the door just a crack about a minute later, shoved the game out the door, and said, 'Here you go—see you in a few days—bye.'"

I coughed. "Did any of that strike Mrs. Lakie as unusual?"

"Nope. But if you knew the Lakies, you'd know that they're used to weird behavior."

"Didn't you tell Mrs. Lakie what was going on?" Nerissa asked.

"I was kind of speechless for a few minutes, but as soon as I regained control of my tongue, I told Mrs. Lakie, 'That's not my Daddy! That's an imposter!'"

"And...she didn't believe you?" I guessed.

"No! She just smiled and said, 'Oh sweetie, that's your father. You just don't recognize him without the beard.' I tried to explain, but she wouldn't take me seriously."

I groaned in annoyance. "It's what I call Snuffleupagus Syndrome."

Daisy looked confused. "What's that?"

"Well, this was decades ago, long before you were born. Today, everybody knows that Mr. Snuffleupagus is real on *Sesame Street*, but earlier in the show's run, Big Bird was the only character with any contact with Snuffy. That's why all the adults on the show thought that Snuffy was just Big Bird's imaginary friend. They figured that there was no way they could miss an enormous mammoth-like creature, and it became a running gag how Snuffy left the area right before someone else came by. Then, a bunch of people complained that the show was teaching kids that adults wouldn't believe them if they ever came to them with a serious problem. So they had a Very Special Episode where it was revealed that Snuffy was real, and everybody realized that Big Bird was telling the truth all along, and today, most young viewers of the show have no idea that for years, the adults on *Sesame Street* thought that Snuffy was imaginary."

"Oh." Daisy seemed only mildly interested in the history of children's educational programming, but I realized that her concerns over her own problems were paramount with her right now.

"Hadn't Mrs. Lakie ever met your father before? Didn't you have a photo to show them?" Nerissa queried.

"No. Neither Mrs. Lakie or Alexis ever saw Daddy before. He doesn't come to school often. And I forgot to mention this. Normally, our living room's filled with pictures of me and Daddy, but last night every photo with Daddy in it was missing. And I didn't have another picture of the two of us with me."

"So someone's making darned sure you can't

prove the guy claiming to be your father is a fraud," I mused.

Daisy looked indescribably grateful. "So, you believe me then?"

"I certainly do."

"So do I," added Nerissa.

"That's great. Thank you." For the first time, a little ray of relief passed over Daisy's face. "So, what do we do now?"

I coughed gently. "*You* go back to class and let us look into this. We'll make our inquiries and we'll get back to you later on today. O.K.?"

Daisy looked a little mutinous, and it was obvious that she wanted to join us on our investigation. She had given up her recess to come to my office and tell me about her worries, and who could blame her for being freaked out and wanting quick results?

"Nerissa, what's your schedule for this afternoon?"

"It's a light day—Let me call Dad. I think he can take over one of my classes, and I can tell the one class to watch a documentary DVD I leave out for them, and the study hall can look after itself."

"So you're coming with me to investigate?"

"Hell, yeah. Some kid's father gets swapped out with an imposter, I'm not going to sit around in a classroom all day while you find out what happened to him." Helping me investigate isn't part of Nerissa's official job description, but I work better with her by my side.

We took a few minutes to work out a plan. Daisy had come to us during late-morning recess, the first opportunity she was free to escape from the watchful eye of her teacher, Miss Dirchity. It was now 11:30.

My initial investigation was hampered by the fact that I didn't know where to find Daisy's father and stepmother. The simplest solution was to call his office and ask, although a little subterfuge was clearly necessary. If we were to call his office and ask where Mr. Ottovorde was supposed to be at the moment, it was conceivably likely that we'd be stonewalled. It's been my experience that wealthy businessmen's offices are trained not to provide any more information about the big boss's location than is absolutely necessary.

After the second ring, a young, female voice said, "Hello, this is the Ottovorde Company. This is Maddie speaking."

Nerissa held up a finger, indicating that she was going to handle the conversation. I was fine with that. I figured the receptionist would respond more helpfully to another woman. Nerissa raised her voice an octave above her normal speaking tone and added a ditzy lilt that is completely foreign to her natural personality.

"Hi… Maddie? Are you Mr. Ottovorde's secretary?"

"Yes, I am. At least, I'm one of his secretaries. Who is this, please?"

"Oh, I'm so sorry. So rude of me. Gosh, I don't know where my head is today. Everything's been going wrong, and if I don't fix this I'm gonna get fired. My name's Jacqueline." Technically, since that's Nerissa's middle name, it wasn't exactly a lie. "And I work for Cuthbertson Hall, you know, the school that Mr. Ottovorde's daughter Daisy goes to."

"Oh, yes. Hi, Jacqueline. What's wrong and how can I help you?"

"Well, I'm so embarrassed. I'm so glad you can't see me right now because I'm blushing so hard I look like a strawberry. Anyway, Mr. Ottovorde sent a letter to Cuthbertson Hall, I think it's about a donation he or someone in his family made recently or in the past, I don't know, I didn't get to read it. I'm such a klutz! I knocked my coffee cup over, and soaked the letter, and now it's unreadable and I have no idea what it said. And I'm already in trouble with my supervisor because I accidentally bumped the table and sent a bowl of hot soup right into his lap at lunch, and if he finds out I made that stupid mistake with the coffee and the letter he's going to fire me, I just know it..." At this point Nerissa broke into sobs. I was both impressed by her acting ability and praying that she would never pull a similar emotional manipulation on me.

"Jacqueline, are you all right?"

Between tears, Nerissa managed to choke out the words, "Yes. No. I don't know. If only I could talk to Mr. Ottovorde and ask him what he wrote in that letter. Then it would be all right. I know that if I had just two minutes to speak to him and explain..."

There was a pause, and then Maddie said, "Listen, honey, don't worry about it. Mr. Ottovorde's a demanding boss, but he's not a bad guy at all. And he can't bear watching a woman cry. I know because one time I lost control of my car in the parking lot and dented his back fender, so I came right to him and sobbed and begged him not to fire me, and after five minutes and about a gallon's worth of tears, he told me not to worry about it, and even gave me an extra half-hour for lunch that day. I'm sure if you talk to him, and make sure to cry long and loud, he'll tell you what was in that letter."

Nerissa grabbed a tissue from the box on my desk and started sponging away her crocodile tears. "But where is he? I've no idea where to find him."

"Hang on a sec." After the sound of a keyboard clicking, Maddie replied, "In about fifteen minutes he's going to have lunch at the Grandidierite Club. He's got a business meeting with his wife and some potential investors. I don't think you'll be able to get into the restaurant—they don't let you in unless you're a member or a guest of a member, but afterwards he's going back to his home to get some rest—he hasn't been feeling well lately."

"Oh, no. Is he all right?"

"I guess so. I haven't seen him in a few days—he's been communicating with me by phone, so I'm not sure what kind of mood he's in today. Do you have his address?"

"Uh, yeah. It's on file here on the school database."

"O.K. He should be home by two-thirty or three. Would you mind not telling him that I told you..."

"Oh, of course not. Thank you, thank you, thank you..." After a few more expressions of gratitude, Nerissa hung up the phone and shot me a smile filled with self-satisfied triumph.

"Well done, Nerissa."

"Thanks. Would it be vain for me to say how proud I am of myself?"

"Not at all—I'm proud of you, too."

"As well you should be." Nerissa flipped an extremely long stray strand of her dark brown mane out her face. "So, what's the plan? We're not members at the Grandidierite Club, and if we hide outside the wall, security's gonna bust us."

"True…" I reflected upon the geography of the general North Shore of Milwaukee area, and then remembered something. "But the Winding Road is right across the river from the Grandidierite, remember?"

The Winding Road is a tiny bar and restaurant catering to motorcyclists. The Grandidierite Club has been trying to shut the place down for years, claiming the noise of the motorcycles upsets their members, but so far the Winding Road has survived, partly because their clientele has one of the few segments of Milwaukee society able to intimidate the city's wealthiest residents.

Nerissa's face lit up. "Give me five minutes to clear my schedule for the afternoon, and I'll meet you at the garage."

About a year ago, I managed to clear one of my students after she was falsely accused of murder. In gratitude, her father, who owns a motorcycle shop, gave me and Nerissa a pair of beautiful Harley-Davidsons. We both love riding, but Nerissa's mother is not a fan of motorcycles, due to a family tragedy involving one. So we keep the Harleys in a quiet corner of the garage used to store the Cuthbertson school buses, and we take them out from time to time, and enjoy our racing in relative secret.

Five minutes later, I was hanging up my suit and tie in my locker at the garage, and pulling on a black T-shirt, and my black leather cycling jacket and matching pants. I pulled the tarp off of our bikes, and shortly afterwards Nerissa joined me, wearing her one-piece red and black leather racing suit.

"What do you think is happening with Daisy's father?" Nerissa asked, pulling on her gloves.

Lacing up my left boot, which had come untied, I replied, "I haven't got enough evidence to craft a solid theory, but something kind of messed up needs to be happening if a little girl's being told that a man she's never met before is her father... but my gut tells me that Mr. Ottovorde isn't in danger."

"No offense, but your gut's been wrong before."

"Yes, it has. But the thing is, this is pretty clumsy. Mr. Ottovorde's relatively well-known in Milwaukee. There's a couple of hundred people who could take one glance at him and say, 'Hey! Daisy's right! That's not Doug Ottovorde! What the hell are you trying to pull here?'"

"Well, we know his wife is involved somehow, but we don't know why she's doing what she is or just how malicious her intent is."

"Right, but we can make a pretty shrewd guess as to her motive." I tossed Nerissa's helmet to her and picked up my own. "The Ottovordes are really, really rich. When there's that much money around, the reason for whatever's going on is bound to be connected to cold hard cash."

And with that, we hopped onto our motorcycles and sped to the Winding Road in just under four minutes. I was a bit disappointed our journey was over so soon, because I was just beginning to enjoy my ride, but I had an investigation to perform, and I didn't have time to take a few more laps around the block.

I'd never been to the Winding Road before, though I knew all about its reputation as a biker bar. I had thought that being dressed as we were would help us blend in better, but once again I realized I hadn't done enough to gather background information about my destination. Despite our motorcycling leathers we both stood out from the crowd. I was the only clean-shaven guy there, and also the most neatly groomed, despite my helmet messing up my hair. After taking one quick breath through my nose, I realized I also probably had better hygiene than any of the other guys there. And most eyes in the room were on Nerissa, as she was by a couple of country miles the youngest, prettiest, and slimmest woman there.

The bartender greeted us gruffly but pleasantly enough, and at my request, showed us over to the outdoor deck overlooking the water. We maneuvered him over to the corner of the deck closest to the Grandidierite Club, and as we sat down, he slapped a couple of torn, creased, and stained menus in front of us.

When you're observing someone, you have to be ready to go at a moment's notice so you can't wait too long for your food or to pay. My mentor in the P.I. business taught me to always order soup, because it takes no time to prepare or serve.

"Two bowls of your chili, please. With seltzer water to drink, and the check right away, please." Normally, Nerissa would have some very sharp words for me if I ordered for her without consulting her, but she knows the drill—on a case, our meals tend to come in a bowl and are eaten with a spoon.

The bartender grunted and lurched away, and I

whipped out my pocket binoculars and started scanning the deck of the Grandidierite Club.

"You know, they may not even be outside," Nerissa noted. "There's a chilly breeze."

"I know, but—" I nearly dropped my binoculars in excitement. "Nerissa! Pass me the camera, please!"

Nerissa's hand darted into her enormous purse, rummaged for a few seconds, and withdrew with my camera with the miniature telescopic lens. I snapped a dozen quick photos, stopping only when my targets slipped behind a grove of trees, out of sight.

I clicked more buttons, and showed Nerissa the camera's tiny digital screen. "Take a look."

She peered at the photo, then whipped out her phone, tapped her thumbs repeatedly so fast they were just a blur, and showed me a picture from the website of a prominent local magazine, depicting the genuine Mr. and Mrs. Ottovorde at a fancy Christmas charity party from last year. "That's definitely Brielle on the Grandidierite Club deck now, but the man whose arm she's on is not her husband, Doug."

"No, it isn't." Comparing my recently-taken photos with the online image, it was clear that this mystery man was a few inches taller, about thirty pounds leaner, and twenty years younger than the real Doug Ottovorde, not to mention the point that Daisy had told us about earlier—he didn't have a beard. Plus the mystery man had no gray hairs.

At this point, the bartender arrived, serving us—or rather, slamming our chili and drinks down in front of us with such force that I was surprised to see that the bowls and glasses didn't crack or chip. He yanked a handful of saltine cracker packets out of his apron pocket and tossed them carelessly to the table, and then slapped the bill down next to me. Having seen the prices on the menu, I was prepared, and handed him a ten dollar bill, along with a friendly "keep the change." If our server felt any gratitude whatsoever, I could not discern one atom of it from his facial expression.

I crushed three packets of crackers, tore them open, sprinkled them in my chili, and then, after a quick stir, tasted it. I'm very fond of spicy food, but I'd never had anything like this before. This was a combination of Carolina Reaper peppers, nitroglycerine, and Jeeves' morning mixtures as described by P.G. Wodehouse. After one bite, I wasn't sure if I still had a tongue. The Scoville Heat Unit level must have measured in the trillions. I gulped my seltzer, realized, that the chili was probably going to play merry havoc with my digestive system, and then decided the hell with it—this was the best chili I'd ever had. I put away several more spoonfuls before I noticed that Nerissa's face had turned the color of ketchup.

"This is way too spicy," she wheezed.

"Do you want me to finish that for you?"

She waved away my eager spoon. "I didn't say I wasn't enjoying it."

As I was scraping my bowl clean, I remembered that I was supposed to be keeping an eye on the Grandidierite Club. I picked up my binoculars, scanned the general area, and once again located my quarry. I grabbed the camera and took a few more photos.

After chugging down the last of her seltzer, Nerissa asked, "Did you get anything good?"

"I think so." I showed her the pictures. "Look at this. Brielle and Not-Doug Ottovorde are shaking hands with three people in business suits."

"The three investors Daisy met at her house?"

"That's a safe bet. Take a look at this one. If I zoom in, we can get a look at a symbol on a binder one of them is carrying." I tapped buttons until I could make out the words "Annulus Corporation."

"Half a sec." Nerissa wiped her lips on a paper napkin and exercised her skill with search engines. "It's a European outfit specializing in a lot of the same fields as the Ottovorde Company. According to a financial news story from three months ago, they're looking at expanding their operations into the United States. So if they're looking for a merger or a buyout or some sort of business partnership… the Ottovorde Company would be a likely choice to work with, at least as far as I can tell."

"Hmmm…." As I was mentally digesting this information, I took another look through the binoculars. "It looks like the five of them are going inside the club for lunch. I doubt I'll be able to get another good look at them for at least another an hour and a half or so."

"Sounds about right," Nerissa nodded. "So, what do we do now? Sit and wait?"

I considered this prospect for a second. I was seriously considering ordering another bowl of chili, but my brain abruptly overruled my stomach. "Let's think about it. Brielle Ottovorde is currently with a man—presumably the same one Daisy met last night—"

"That's a fair assumption, but it's not certain," Nerissa noted.

"You're right. We need to confirm this with the witness."

And with that, the two of us walked back to our motorcycles and sped back to Cuthbertson

Hall. Once we were back, I texted Miss Tommers, the Lower School secretary, asking her to take Daisy out of class and bring her to her office. A few seconds after we arrived at Miss Tommers' empty office, she returned with Daisy in tow.

"Thanks so much, Miss Tommers."

"You're welcome, Funderburke. What's going on?"

"It's our belief that Daisy's father has been replaced with an imposter."

"Oh, dear!"

"That's not for public knowledge, by the way." I showed Daisy the camera screen. "Is this the man you saw at your house last night? The one who claimed to be your father?"

Daisy nodded vigorously. "Yes! That's the imposter!"

"And these three people," I tapped my camera buttons. "Are those the other three individuals you saw—"

She didn't even let me finish. "They are! They are!"

"What are you talking about?" Miss Tommers asked.

"Daisy can tell you the whole story in a few minutes," Nerissa explained.

I kept processing the facts of the case in my

mind. "Obviously, some sort of deception is going on here. But it's not a very clever one. Anybody familiar with Doug Ottovorde would know..." I looked at Daisy. "Those silly adults wouldn't listen to you because they didn't believe a child. We need an adult who knows your father who no one will contradict, like—"

"Your grandmother," Nerissa and I said together. Nerissa has a habit of cutting in on some of my big moments.

"Where's your grandmother now?" I asked Daisy. "At her house?" I said "house," but I knew it was really more of a mansion.

"No, she's been staying at the Trillium Terrace for the last month and a half," Daisy corrected me. "She had a hip replacement a while ago, and there were complications, so she's been at that nursing home where she has constant care. She hates it there," Daisy added. "I talked to her on the phone the other day, and she says she's going to go stark raving mad if she has to spend another day in God's waiting room."

"Do you know what her room number is?"

"Yes. 123."

I smiled. "Easy number to remember."

"It's supposed to be a luxury suite. Grandma said that if she had to be a prisoner at an old person's home, she might as well be as comfortable as possible. But she says it's completely unlivable. She had to buy a new living room set because she didn't have a comfortable place to sit. And she doesn't trust the staff there. Before he left on his trip, she had Daddy lock all her jewelry away in a safety deposit box, because she was sure the employees were just waiting for their chance to plunder her valuables."

Nerissa smiled. "Well if Mrs. Wilhelmina Ottovorde says that the man claiming to be Doug Ottovorde isn't her son at all, she'll make darned sure that everybody listens to her and believes her."

Daisy started to jump with excitement. "Why didn't I think of that! I should've told Mrs. Lakie to call Grandma last night!"

"Well, a slight delay isn't going to cause any serious problems." I pulled out my phone and looked up the location of the Trillium Terrace. It was only a mile and a half away. "I think we should have a word with your grandmother. If we're lucky, we may be able to confront your stepmother and the imposter before they finish their dessert."

"Brielle doesn't eat dessert. She says sugar is as bad as arsenic, and she doesn't want me having any sweets either."

I was already inclined to see Brielle as a cold-hearted villainess, and denying dessert to a little girl did nothing to endear her to me. "Well, no time to waste. Daisy, please tell Miss Tommers the whole story, and with a little luck, we should be able to resolve the situation by the end of the school day."

And with that, Nerissa and I returned to the parking lot, climbed back on our motorcycles, and zoomed off to Trillium Terrace. The moment we arrived, I realized that we'd made a tactical error. I'd suggested riding our motorcycles in order to blend in better at the Winding Road, but it wasn't really necessary. If I'd driven my Volvo to the biker bar and worn my usual suit, the result wouldn't have been any different.

But the Trillium Terrace was different. I could see through the big glass doors that the front desk was well-staffed, and the men there did not look like mere receptionists, but like ex-military men working security. You didn't stay at the Trillium if you don't have plenty of money, and a place that charges high enough fees to make Cuthbertson Hall's tuition look downright cheap was bound to be pretty selective about who they let in and who they didn't. If our names weren't on an approved list, we weren't likely to get inside. And motorcycling leathers would do nothing to help you blend in at a posh retirement home.

It was as if Nerissa were reading my mind. "Funderburke, I just had an unsettling idea. What if don't let us in, and they call Brielle Ottovorde to let her know that two strangers wanted to see her mother-in-law?"

That further complicated matters. I took a long, slow, deep breath to ponder the matter...and smelled cigarette smoke. "C'mon," I told Nerissa, leading her around the side of the building.

My nose had come to our rescue. As I suspected, a couple of employees in nursing scrubs were sitting on a wall smoking, and they had left a side door propped open. It was easy for us to sneak behind them quietly and slip into the building unobserved.

After five minutes of wrong turns and scrambling to stay out of the sight of residents, we finally found ourselves in front of room 123. I knocked, and a magisterial woman's voice responded, "Come in, but make your visit brief. I'm about to settle down for my nap."

I pushed open the door, and as we entered, Mrs. Wilhelmina Ottovorde looked us up and down disapprovingly. "I knew this rest home wasn't up to par, but I didn't think I'd be subject to a burglary from a biker gang."

I made a calculated decision to ignore that comment. "Mrs. Ottovorde, I'm Isaiah Funderburke and this is Nerissa Kaiming. We work for Cuthbertson Hall—"

"Are you here to ask for money? Because I just donated funds for a library reading room to Cuthbertson last fall."

I was aware of this. The new Ottovorde Reading Room went great with the Ottovorde Tennis Court, the Ottovorde Chemistry Lab, the Ottovorde Choir Room, and the Ottovorde Photography Studio.

"No, we're here at the request of your granddaughter, Daisy." And before Mrs. Ottovorde could interrupt me again, I immediately launched into the whole story of her son being replaced with an imposter.

Perhaps my storytelling skills kept her speechless, because Mrs. Ottovorde didn't say a word until a full ten seconds after I concluded my narrative. "I have never trusted that Brielle," she sniffed decisively. "All bosoms and no character."

"So will you help us?" Nerissa asked. "If you could come with us and confront them—"

"Of course."

"I'll call for a rideshare."

"Young man, why would you need to do that?"

She paused. "Oh, did you two ride the same motorcycle here?"

"No, we each have our own—"

"Then there's no problem." Mrs. Ottovorde rose with considerable enthusiasm. "Mr. Funderburke, I shall ride with you."

Nerissa and I raised the sort of objections one might expect. They had no effect on Mrs. Ottovorde. To be honest, I wasn't trying very hard to convince her otherwise. My thoughts on the matter were as follows:

CON: This senior citizen has just had a hip replacement. She could conceivably fall off my motorcycle and be seriously injured. If anything happened to a wealthy donor, my position at the school could be in jeopardy.

PRO: I liked the old lady's spirit. Plus I wanted to see her reaction to the ride.

"Have you ever ridden as a passenger on a motorcycle before?" I asked.

"Not since I was nineteen."

"Do you have a helmet?" Nerissa inquired.

"No." Mrs. Ottovorde looked a bit disappointed. "Will that be a problem?"

"It's a safety matter, and just plain common sense," I replied.

Mrs. Ottovorde thought for a moment. "There's a janitor here who rides a motorcycle to work. I saw him arrive just a few minutes ago. He leaves his helmet dangling from the handlebars. I'm sure he won't mind if we borrowed it for a couple of hours without asking." She gestured to Nerissa. "Dear, please hand me my coat from the closet there. The olive green one."

Nerissa obligingly retrieved a coat that looked a lot like one that Helen Mirren wore in *The Queen*. I helped Mrs. Ottovorde into it, and then picked her up and carried her out of the room, across the hall, and down a stairwell, with Nerissa getting the doors for us. I had briefly considered placing Mrs. Ottovorde in a wheelchair, but the elevator was in a public area, and I thought the risk of being caught was too great. Two minutes later, I gently set her on the back of my Harley while Nerissa "borrowed" the janitor's helmet.

This is definitely not the smartest thing I've ever done, I thought to myself as I pulled out of the parking lot with Mrs. Ottovorde's arms around me. After a few moments of reflection, I realized that I didn't care. I did take care to go at least fifteen miles per hour slower than I normally would have as we made our way to the Grandidierite Club. Nerissa is not in the habit of tempering her speed for any reason, so she beat us there by a couple of minutes, though it didn't do her much good. When Mrs. Ottovorde and I arrived, Nerissa was exchanging some heated words with the guard at the gate, who apparently refused to let her inside.

Mrs. Ottovorde removed her helmet. "Jason! That young lady and this gentleman are my guests. Treat them accordingly."

The guard's eyes bulged, and after a moment he gurgled something that could conceivably have been an apology, and unlocked the gate.

"Did you enjoy the ride?" I asked her as I gently lifted her off the bike.

"Very much. It's been a long time since I took a journey with a nice young biker."

I would have preferred that she had said "a *handsome* young biker," but I have too much dignity to fish for compliments. Within a minute the three of us were inside the restaurant lobby, and Mrs. Ottovorde informed the concierge that he was to bring Doug and Brielle Ottovorde out to meet her immediately, but he was only to inform them that this was an emergency. He was not to tell them the name of the person demanding an audience, only to tell them to come at once. After Mrs. Ottovorde requested and received permission to use the concierge's private office, the three of us took seats inside the little room while the concierge relayed the message.

Within moments, the concierge led a confused-looking young couple inside the office.

"Thank you. Please leave us and shut the door," Mrs. Ottovorde ordered. The concierge complied, and the millisecond the door closed she boomed, "WHAT THE HELL ARE YOU UP TO AND WHAT HAVE YOU DONE TO MY SON?"

Brielle and the ersatz Doug Ottovorde crumbled like shortbread under a sledgehammer. "I...I...I..." Brielle stammered. "It's n-not what you think."

"DON'T TELL ME WHAT I THINK! TELL ME WHAT'S GOING ON!"

Normally, I like to ask the questions when confronting suspects, but at the moment I was having way too much fun to care.

"He's all right!" the fake Doug informed us. "We didn't do anything to him. We're trying to help him and the company."

"What's your real name?" I asked him. Wilhelmina Ottovorde was doing a pretty impressive job interrogating them, but I can't stay on the sidelines for long.

"I'm Jerry Cossins. I'm Brielle's half-brother."

I believed him, and that shattered the theory that Brielle was trying to replace her husband with a more age-appropriate boyfriend. I only saw a slight resemblance, though the half-sibling relationship probably explained that.

Mrs. Ottovorde moderated her vocal volume. "Tell me what's going on. Now!"

Brielle started stammering again. "We...c-c-c-can't."

"Why the h-h-h-h-h-hell not?" Mrs. Ottovorde mocked her.

"We p-p-p-promised Doug we wouldn't let you know what happened to him." Brielle and Jerry clamped their mouths together and shifted uncomfortably.

"Don't be ridiculous. Explain yourselves!"

As time passed and the half-siblings maintained their silence, I decided to step in and try to provoke a response.

"Let's consider what we know," I said. "Brielle and the real Doug went to Europe. When Brielle returned, the real Doug wasn't with her. Brielle just said she was trying to help the company, she didn't harm Doug, and that they promised not to tell his mother what was going on. It sounds to me that Doug is the architect of his own impersonation."

"That's true," Jerry chimed in. "This was all Doug's idea." His half-sister elbowed him, but I felt like I was on a roll and decided to press them further.

"If Doug can't come himself, that means that he's indisposed. I can think of two possibilities. The first is that he injured himself in some embarrassing way, and that he's stuck in the hospital and unable to take care of the business negotiations because he's physically incapable of doing so. It could've happened like that, but I think the second option is way more likely."

"What's the second option?" Nerissa asked.

"Doug is in prison and doesn't want his mother and would-be business partners to know."

"Yes!" Brielle's stubborn face melted, and I knew I'd hit a home run. "How did you know?"

"I didn't know for certain, it just sounded like a reasonable explanation for why a man would get another guy to pretend to be him for a while."

"Tell us the whole story." Mrs. Ottoborne pursed her lips.

This time, Brielle obliged. "We were in Europe, setting up the early negotiations for the business deal. Everything went really well at our meetings, and Doug and I went to a bar to have a drink to celebrate. Then some sleazy-looking guy stumbled up to me, said something vile, and groped me. Doug hit him, the two started fighting, and the next thing I know, I'm in a courtroom and a judge is sentencing Doug to a month in jail for disturbing the peace."

"Why didn't my son hire the best lawyer he could find?"

"Because he was afraid that if he fought it, it would get into the newspapers and the scandal would lead to the deal falling through. We'd never met the business partners who were coming to Milwaukee before, so Doug came up with the idea of asking Jerry to play him for a while."

"I'm an actor," Jerry explained. "I just finished playing Ben in *The Sunshine Boys* in Chicago. I'm a natural blond, but I dyed my hair brown. We decided not to use a false beard or aging makeup because it might've been spotted. So I mimicked Doug's voice, and I tried to really capture his character by—"

Mrs. Ottovorde held up a hand. "Save it, Olivier. Brielle, keep going."

"Well, everything worked really well. We didn't tell you we were back in town, and when the European investors came to Milwaukee we all got along really well, and then Daisy showed up. We panicked, but fortunately none of them seemed to suspect anything. They thought that Daisy just didn't recognize her dad without the beard."

"Foolish of them," I noted.

"Well, we just kept going, and everything went perfectly. They're leaving tonight. We've got all the details of the deal worked out, and we just signed the papers."

"But wouldn't the contract be invalid if Jerry signed instead of Doug?" Nerissa asked.

"Jerry didn't sign. I did. I have the authority given my position in the company." Brielle flushed. "I know you think I'm a floozy and a gold digger, Wilhelmina, but it may interest you to know that I really do love your son. I know the rumors about me, but I've never been a showgirl or a stripper or a hooker. Doug met me at a business meeting. I'm a pretty good negotiator, and he was attracted to me because of my business skills."

I was pretty sure that there were other reasons for his attraction besides her talent for finance, but I thought it would be ungentlemanly to say so.

"So that's it. This deal is going to make the Ottovorde Company tens of millions over the next decade. It's a triumph for us, but it never would've happened if they'd heard about Doug's conviction.

They'll probably let him out in another week or so for good behavior, and then he'll quietly travel back home, and I'll handle most of the face-to-face negotiations with our new partners in the future, but if necessary I'll get Jerry to reprise the role of Doug, and if we can just keep them from finding out about the deception for a few months it'll be too late for them to back out, so there!" Brielle flushed and paused for breath. "So there, you see? We haven't done anything wrong!"

"You scared the hell out of a six-year-old girl—your own stepdaughter," I reminded her.

Brielle bit her lip. "I feel bad about that."

"Well, you'd better find a way to make that up to her."

"I will, I will. I know I haven't been much of a stepmother to her, but I want to fix that." Brielle sighed. "May we please get back to our new partners? They'll be wondering where we are."

I nodded, and then realized to my chagrin that Brielle and Jerry weren't looking at me for approval. The half-siblings turned and started to walk through the door. As they exited, Mrs. Ottovorde called out, "We shall have a very long conversation in the future, Brielle."

Brielle flinched, but said nothing.

Left alone in the room, Mrs. Ottovorde sighed

and turned to us. "I'm very grateful to you both for how you've handled this situation."

"Think nothing of it, Mrs. Ottovorde," Nerissa replied.

"Call me Mina."

We did, and Mina smiled. "I will show you some proper gratitude in the near future, I just need time to think of something suitable. But in return I'm going to ask you to do something else for me, please."

"Of course," I said.

"Just name it," Nerissa added.

A twinkle appeared in Mina's eyes. "Take me for another motorcycle ride from time to time, will you?"

I couldn't stop myself from laughing, and neither could Nerissa. When I was finally able to speak again I answered Mina with an enormous smile. "It's a deal."

"Do you want me to go shopping with you for your own motorcycle suit?" Nerissa asked.

Mina looked thoughtful. "I wonder if we can find one like yours, only in black and green. Green has always been my favorite color…"

DIRK KNIGHT AND THE MOVING VAN VIOLATION

JASON A. ADAMS

The city never sleeps.

From Roswell to Jonesboro, from Smyrna to Stone Mountain. Atlanta hums and roars twenty-five hours a day.

The city has seen its share of movie stars, moguls, and mobsters. Saints and sinners living, loving, and dying in the mosquito-filled swampy air of this global hub of humanity.

Most people in the ATL are decent folk who mind their manners and do their jobs. But, as with any mixed barrel, sometimes a rotten apple gets down in the middle of things and causes a spreading blight of trouble.

That's when the good citizens of Atlanta call on—

Dirk Knight, Private Eye.

Monday. 10:34 AM. Already the heavy July heat and humidity blanketed the city like microwaved molasses. Even the bugs kept their summer racket down to a low, lazy buzz.

Jerry Farnsworth, licensed investigator, leaned back from the harsh glow of a pair of twenty-four-inch LED monitors, rubbing his eyes. He was on his third background check of the day, and already bored to tears.

Traffic tickets. Credit card defaults. Friends or family in trouble with the law. And those were the exciting parts of corporate hiring investigations.

He slid open a desk drawer, pawed through until he found what he was hoping for. One lonely foil-wrapped reesie cup, carefully hidden away for an emergency.

Mid-unwrap, Jerry paused. The drool-inducing aromas of fresh shrimp, plump yeast rolls, and broiling vegetables floated through the room, reminding him that Barb was counting on him to taste test some of her new recipes.

Oh well. *One* little reesie wouldn't spoil his dinner. Not for Barb's cooking. He kept one eye on the door that led from their office/living room to the kitchen and popped the chocolate, chewing faster than it deserved.

Things had certainly changed for Jerry since last year. From an unemployed computer nerd-turned-private eye to a fully incorporated, licensed background checker and skip tracer. From a loser living in his mom's house to a happily settled family man, living with his first client-turned-girlfriend.

Last summer, Barb had come to Dirk Knight, Jerry's PI fantasy alter-ego, for help with her ex-partner and some pilfered recipes. He hadn't been able to do much, except suggest that she focus more on branding than originality, and thus the Barb's Dream line of salad dressings had been born. Atlanta likes few things better than good food or good jokes, so the line took off like one of the big Delta jets that called the city home.

Between Barb's condiment kingdom and his own internet prowess, their two businesses had allowed them to shack up in a fairly nice Decatur shack, buy a couple of new used cars that had some good life left in them, and keep the lights on. Dirk Knight, Private Eye hadn't gone anywhere, but Jerry Farnsworth, Background Checker made a decent living.

A few parts of his old life had come with them. Barb's kitchen was full of gleaming stainless appliances, sparkling black stone composite countertops, and a rack of wicked Japanese cutlery any samurai chef would die for. That was her kingdom, and she ruled with an iron fist.

Dirk's office—while sharing the floral wallpaper and drapes that Barb had picked out for the apartment—held his battered old oak desk, the antique office chair that had mercifully lost its shriek after a good refurbishing and a gallon of oil, and the classic black rotary desk phone. Only good for incoming calls in this age of touch-tone everything, but...

But.

Only one phone number rang to that phone. And not for background checks or bail hoppers.

He'd promised Barb he wouldn't give up on Dirk Knight, and he hadn't. However, the world seemed to have given up on him.

Someday...

He still had trouble believing the beautiful Barbara Collins wanted to share his life. An inch taller than his own five-nine, better curves than a Greg Maddux slow pitch, and the best cook—no, *chef*—he'd ever met. His mom's salmon patties didn't stand a chance against her butter-roasted sea bass.

She'd even helped him work on his fitness. Although he had to keep *that* little secret from her. The guy she'd hired him to investigate, her old partner Maurice Kadnes, had handed Jerry's ass to him on a shiny white catering platter the first time they met. But he wasn't a bad sort, and Jerry had to admit he'd started the fight. Maurice disagreed a little with Barb over who had come up with certain recipes, but that didn't stop him from offering to tutor her new boyfriend in Tae Kwon Do for fifty bucks a lesson.

After four months Jerry wasn't any kind of

master, but he could at least touch his toes. And break a few boards. Not that he expected to be attacked by a gang of one-by-twelves from the local lumber yard, but it was a pretty nifty trick.

Pity that living with Barb and her cooking meant he'd only tightened his belt one notch.

He rubbed his eyes again, took a swig of diet coke to wash the peanut butter from his tongue, and reached for the mouse. Time to see if Libby Carlson, hopeful applicant for *Tony's Shop 'n Save*, had any priors in her eighteen years of living.

Barb just *adored* the way Jerry's eyes closed and his chewing slowed down. What better way to know that her *crevettes à l'ail flamboyant* had hit the mark? A few more like this and she'd be ready to rent a little restaurant space. Maybe in Virginia-Highlands, maybe over near Ansley.

She couldn't wait to see his face when she brought out the peanut butter pie. She'd pestered Mrs. Farnsworth for her mother's recipe, and then tweaked it with a richer, darker chocolate ganache and a crust made from crushed chocolate-covered graham crackers.

Jerry wolfed down another dinner roll as she

sashayed back to the kitchen and got the pie out of the fridge to warm for a few minutes.

Just as she got her own plate of the garlic shrimp with the fancy name, a jangling *brrrriiing* split the air. She'd never heard that sound in this apartment, but nothing else in the world sounded like a classic Ma Bell desk phone.

"Don't you *dare!*" she yelled as Jerry tried to jump up from his chair. She'd been waiting a whole year for this moment.

Barb shot past him and into his office. She plunked her butt on the edge of his desk, mindful of the splinters, crossed her ankles and picked up the receiver.

"Dirk Knight Detective Agency," she purred—or at least tried to purr—in the husky, two-octaves-lower voice she'd been watching old Kathleen Turner movies to get right. "Trixie speaking. Can I help you?"

Twining the handset's curly cord in her fingers, she gave Jerry a wink. He leaned against the doorjamb, staring at her with the look of a puppy dog at a sausage explosion.

"Trixie?" said the woman on the other end. "Who is this Trixie? Is that you, Barbara dear? This is Ms. Marshall. Is that nice young man of yours available? I need him to look into something for me."

Barb rolled her eyes and handed the phone to him. "Ms. Marshall, honey. She wants you for a job. A *paying* job!"

She might have said the latter a teeny tiny tad more loudly, to make sure their unpleasant neighbor got the hint.

Jerry took the phone, and immediately morphed into Dirk Knight. He stood up straighter. His eyes took on that steely glint (really, it was steely rather than squinty). He even managed to suck in his belly a little.

He wasn't eating enough. She'd been shirking.

"Ms. Marshall? Knight here. What's that? Where? When? The devil you say. Yes ma'am. A hundred bucks a day plus expenses. No, I don't take cards. Cash only. No...no ma'am. I assure you... yes, that's right. Thank you, Ms. Marshall. I'll get to it right away."

She held her breath as he dropped the receiver back in place. Fingers crossed, she raised her eyebrows.

"She wants me for a case, Barb. A *case!*" He grinned his big, goofy little kid grin.

Barb couldn't help it. She squealed like a little

kid herself, took his hands and danced him around the office.

"That's *wonderful* honey! What's the scoop?"

"A...a moving van..." He stopped to catch his breath. Dancing really wasn't his thing, she knew. "Parked behind the maintenance building at the back of the complex. She says there hasn't been any trouble, but the van keeps rocking a little, like someone's inside. She wants me to make sure no one's been kidnapped or anything. Cops told her she can't call them for a few months, she said."

"Not after the last dozen or so dire emergencies?" she said, unable to stop a snort, not that she tried. "Like the time the Tanakas moved in, or that nice Falcon linebacker had the temerity to get in his own car in broad daylight? I bet if you dig, you'll find her first name really *is* Karen."

His eyes rolled, much as hers had. The Ms. Marshall Effect.

"She said no one will notice if I'm prowling around. Still, it's a hundred dollars and a notch in the belt. What's for dessert? I gotta eat if I'm gonna work."

"Go sit back down, and I'll bring it to you."

Barb dashed to the kitchen, then through the kitchen to the bedroom. A quick change of wardrobe, then back to the kitchen to cut Jer—*Dirk* a slice of pie.

She brought the pie to him held high, wearing his fedora and his tie…and a smile.

"I *do* hope you enjoy your dessert, Mr. Knight."

Dirk walked slowly through the night toward his target.

Not because he was trying to sneak. People trying to sneak usually stood out like sore thumbs. At least in a middle-class apartment complex where a pot of petunias on the stoop made you some kind of tenant rebel.

Nope, he moved slowly because even at eleven PM, the July air held more water than oxygen. And he didn't want to stain his PI shirt any more than necessary.

That, and Barb had worn him plumb out. Whatta woman!

He'd have to start calling her Trixie, but that was okay. Barb and Jerry by day, Trixie and Dirk after dark. He liked it.

The moving van wasn't hard to spot. Right there behind the building where the Schlafly brothers kept all their lawn maintenance and landscaping gear.

A twenty-foot panel van. Ford. Good tires. The marks of a few rust spots professionally filled. A thin scrim of fairly fresh white paint, not quite hiding the logo of a famous DIY rental company.

So far, nothing suspicious at all. Except for the fact that most people in this area would die before doing their own manual labor. *Manuel labor,* Ms. Marshall called it, usually with a disdainful sniff. Never mind the Schlafly brothers were about as Mexican as Taco Bell.

Only a couple more years of careful saving, and he could buy Barb a house. Maybe a small one, but something Marshall-less of their very own.

Hell, he'd make sure they moved to a neighborhood full of The Gays and *those people,* and send Ms. Marshall an engraved invitation to the housewarming.

But first he had to earn his pay.

And Ms. Marshall was right. Every so often, the van rocked on its axles. Not much, but too much for something with no people inside.

Now Dirk sneaked. He lowered into somewhat of a crouch, mindful of the stress on his waistband button. Inched forward one slow sliding step at a time.

A heavy orange cable hung from the bottom of the van, stretching through the grass. He followed it and found the end plugged into a heavy-duty outlet.

Hmmm...

He decided to play it with old-fashioned cool.

"Open up!" he yelled, beating on the van's rear sliding door. "Dirk Knight, Private Eye!"

Inside the van, something clattered and banged, followed by a not very criminal-sounding voice.

"Shit, man. Don't bang the gong so loud. I'm coming, I'm coming."

Dirk stepped back, hand in pocket, thumb poised over his panic siren.

The door slid upward with a huge rattle.

"What's the deal—Jerry? That you, man?"

Dirk's jaw flung itself open.

"Mike? Holy shit, dude! What the hell you doing hiding in a moving truck?"

Mike laughed and jumped down for a heavy round of bro-hugs and back slapping. He wore the same Hawaiian shirt and cargo shorts that had been his uniform back when he and Jerry Farnsworth hopped IT contracts from gig to gig. A little more in need of laundering than in the old days, both the shirt and the skin, but only a little.

"Hey, it's a cheap way to have both an office

and a crash pad," Mike said. "Hop up and I'll give you the grand tour."

Dirk grabbed a hand strap and lugged himself up into the van. Mike pulled the door down, and lights automatically came to life.

"Wow," Dirk said. And he meant it. This place was pretty damn cool.

Along one wall of the eight-by-twenty-foot space ran a long workbench covered with keyboards and monitors. An aluminum rack mounted toward the cab wall held two blade enclosures filled with the blinky-flashies that spoke of high-end computer hardware living its best life. A bright green network cable ran from a rack-mounted router/hub combo up to the ceiling, where what looked a lot like the guts of a DataYanker 3K WiFi receiver were glued to the bright aluminum.

"Whole roof's an antenna, my man," Mike said, with the kind of smug grin only a true geek showing off to another true geek could pull off. "I can pick up the net from just about anywhere. And riding other people's airwaves means The Man can't track me down."

Dirk peeled his drooling eyes away from the tech, noticed a futon against the opposite wall. Took a second look at the organic quality of the mattress, and decided to keep standing.

"Why would The Man want to track you down, dude? What you been into since the reorg?"

Mike had been downsized the same time as Jerry. Jerry had become Dirk, but what had his old friend turned into?

"Oh, a little of this. A little of that." He waved a hand airily.

Dirk went to one of the keyboards on the workbench, typed in a rapid series of keys. The monitors sprang to life, displaying screen after screen of…

"Still haven't changed your password, I—Shit, dude. Seriously?"

The screens were filled with video poker and online slot machines. Except the farthest on the right, which showed two women doing things they probably didn't tell their mothers about. Mike had always had his skeezy side.

"Aw, come on, man," Mike said, hitting the power button on the last monitor as his skin tone edged toward the infrared. "I ain't bad at the poker. Not a millionaire, but I make enough to buy fuel for this beast and myself."

Dirk remembered the extension cord.

"But you're stealing electricity. And hacking networks to get online, right?"

Mike rubbed the back of his neck.

"Well, sure. But these places get a hell of a deal

from the power company on the complex-maintenance juice. And I only hack people who deserve it. Like right now? I'm piggy-backing on this bad broad who's the head of the local UDC. She's evil and a half. You should see the shit she posts on social media about 'heritage' and 'purity' and all that other BS."

UDC. United Daughters of the Confederacy. Proud protectors of good old-fashioned bigotry and better-than-thou-ism.

He already knew, but had to ask.

"So what's this bad broad's name?"

"Marshall," Mike said. "As in Fred Marshall, the Dry Cleaning King."

Of course, it was her. He hadn't known about the connection to the owner of Atlanta's biggest chain of high-end dry cleaners. Besides his laundries, Fred Marshall had a finger in just about everything that the country thought of when it thought of Atlanta. Soft drinks, airlines, TV stations...Fred owned a piece of it all.

Strange that his daughter lived in a nice-but-not-too apartment complex.

He started to ask, but Mike anticipated him.

"Dear old dad chucked her," he said. "She still works for the family biz, but she's not on the family gravy train. From what I found in her email, Pops says she's bad for the family image, what with all the UDC garbage, calling cops on joggers and preachers, deleting large sections of the ozone layer whenever she gets her hair done. Okay, maybe not that last part. Still, she has her MBA and he pays her to keep their books, if not enough to live like a true suthun belle."

"Nah," Dirk said, picturing that bulletproof frosted soccer-mom do. "You're probably right about the hair."

"Now, here's where things get really interesting." Mike hooked a rolling stool out from under the workbench, sat down, and began playing his keyboards like a grungy Liberace. "If you take a look at her personal bank account, and check it against certain payouts Pop's company makes for 'consulting fees,' *and* add that to Pop's less-than-loving emails about how he's not paying her a penny more for the bookkeeping than standard accountant rates..."

"It starts to look a lot like she's taking Dear Old Dad to the cleaners," Dirk finished.

"Yep. So you can see why I don't feel too bad about redistributing some of her bandwidth wealth."

Dirk thought of Penny, a twelve-year-old African-American honor student who'd been humiliated near to death when Ms. Marshall called the police after seeing her commit the heinous sin of knocking on her science project partner's door.

"Can you get enough proof printed out for me to make a phone call? I bet the state and federal tax folks would just *love* to find out about someone practicing creative accounting."

Mike grinned a huge grin and held up his hand for a high five, which Dirk had no problem giving.

"Hell yeah, my man! Let's stick it to The Wo-Man!"

Barb was just *so* proud of Jerry.

She walked down the sidewalk with her arm through his. He wore his full Dirk Knight uniform. Black suit, black tie (a new black tie, the old one had been too wrinkled after the knots), and gray fedora tipped at a jaunty angle.

She'd managed to find a beautiful pink pencil skirt with matching clinch-waisted jacket a la Ingrid Bergman. She also sported a pair of seamed nylons. She felt a little silly only being able to walk from the knees, especially with high heels on, but she adored the look. Bogie and Bergie, on the case.

He'd found the information that horrible Ms.

Marshall wanted, and was on the way to deliver the goods. Wasn't that a delightful phrase? *Deliver the goods.*

Anyway, he hadn't told her what he'd found, no matter how much peanut butter pie she plied him with.

They arrived at Ms. Marshall's petunia-free stoop, and Dirk gave the white wooden door a sharp rat-a-tat with his manly knuckles.

The door opened, and Ms. Marshall tried to give herself eyestrain staring down her nose at her visitors.

"Ah, Jerry. And Barb, how lovely to see you dear. Have you made any progress on that van? Is it full of illegal immigrants hiding from justice? I just know it—"

"No ma'am," Dirk said, raising a hand and cutting her off. "In fact, it's an RV conversion owned by an old friend of mine. I spoke to the complex manager, and cleared the whole thing with her. Mike and his Magic Moving Van will be staying a few days longer, then moving on. There's absolutely no danger to you."

Ms. Marshall fanned herself with one beringed hand. "Well, that certainly is a relief, young man. I do thank you for discovering the truth, although I'm sure no good can come from a homemade camper van like that. But still, I did hire you and I'm sure you'd like to be paid. How much did we say, again?"

"*We* said a hundred dollars," Barb said, putting on her culinary-school-trained Business Woman voice. "Plus expenses. Since there were in fact no expenses, a couple of pictures of Grant will do just fine."

"Oh heavens! *Perish* the thought! I never carry anything with that horrid man's picture on it. The *only* currency I keep on hand is graced with either Mr. Washington or Mr. Jackson. Those two men knew the importance of all of us sticking to our own." She tittered, took a small, rhinestone-studded clutch from a table beside the door, and handed Dirk five twenty dollar bills.

Barb didn't point out that it was *she* who'd asked for payment.

A City of Decatur police car drove through the complex's main gate, and turned to park in front of the building where they stood.

"Ah, I believe your police are here, Ms. Marshall," Dirk said, taking Barb's hand and leading her down the stairs.

"*My* police?" The old busybody's eyebrows were more wrinkled than a shar-pei fresh from the dryer. "*I* certainly haven't called the police today.

What could they want in this neighborhood today?"

Ms. Marshall found out toot-sweet. A handsome young African-American man, tall and strapping in his black uniform, followed by a much smaller Latina with smooth skin and hard eyes moved up the stairs, replacing Dirk and Barb. On the sidewalk, a second man in a suit much like Dirk's stood, holding a shiny leather briefcase and the bored expression of someone who knows exactly where things are going.

"Ms. Marshall?" said the male half of the uniformed pair. Then the woman said, "Ms. *Karen* Marshall? You are under arrest for violating Georgia Code Title 16, Chapter 8, Article 1. You are also being arrested for violating GC 48-7-5."

The briefcased gent on the sidewalk called up. "Don't forget sections 7201 and 7206 of the US Code. That's Federal tax evasion, Ms. Marshall. You'll want a lawyer for the Georgia violations, but a lawyer won't be good for much more than helping you fill out your court forms on the fed stuff. Welcome to IRS Land!"

"My, my, my," Dirk said as Ms. Marshall cursed and spat in a very un-genteel fashion while the police very politely handcuffed her and marched her down to the cruiser. "We should have filmed that.

WeTube needs more videos of white people calling the cops on a Karen."

"I can't believe you didn't *tell* me!" Barb said, punching him in the shoulder. "I could've catered the event!"

"Yeah, my man," said a voice from behind them. Barb turned and saw a rumpled Hawaiian shirt holding up a scruffy and none-too-clean looking guy in cargo shorts. "Hey, thanks for clearing my parking space with your bros in the main office. I owe you, man."

Dirk high-fived the newcomer, then waved toward Barb.

"Mike, meet my girlfriend Barb. Barb, this is Mike. We used to put out fires in IT land. Now, Mike is a Hacker Extraordinaire, with a super-sweet rolling hacker lab."

Then Dirk put his arm around her and squeezed.

"Barb here's a chef. Makes the best damn food on either side of the Perimeter. You gotta come to our place and try these *amazing* fiery garlic shrimp thingies."

He took Barb's arm again, and started back toward their apartment, Mike tagging along behind.

"But you can't have any pie, though. That's all mine, dude."

Mike laughed. "No prob, my man. Say, you thought about the food truck thing? Everybody loves those. My uncle owns a couple of Y'all Haul franchises, and always has some old rides for sale, cheap. I wouldn't take 'em cross country, but they're plenty good for a stove and a fridge."

The possibilities flooded through Barb. Not exactly the *Chez Barb* she hoped to have someday, but a food truck would be a start, and would get her name out there. Dirk would probably get some buzz from helping the police, and the IRS bust of dear deplorable Ms. Marshall.

Maybe their dreams would both get a jump start from this sordid business.

She took her arm back. Put it around Dirk's waist instead.

"Mike," she said. "This feels like the beginning of a beautiful friendship."

Dirk's laugh warmed her belly as they walked up the steps to their own front door.

NOT DEAD YET

ANNIE REED

Marty pegged the two punks for what they were right away.

He didn't want to. He'd stopped by Rosita's place for a quiet meal and was just digging into his lunch—two fish tacos, refried beans, rice—when the two punks walked in the front door like they owned the place. But some things just came naturally, like breathing.

Like keeping an eye out for what was going on in the world around you.

Like recognizing danger when it interrupted your meal.

Rosita's husband always grilled the fish to perfection with just the right amount of spice to liven things up. Sure, Marty would rather have a burger. Her husband served up a two-patty number complete with cheese and a sour pickle, bacon if you asked for it. But Marty's doctor told him he had to cut down on the fat if he didn't want to end up in the hospital, or maybe dead.

The joys of getting old. Just when you thought you'd earned the right to do whatever you wanted, someone came around to tell you that you couldn't.

Marty figured if he had to add fish to his diet, and his doctor said he did, the only kind of fish he was going to eat were the fish tacos at Rosita's.

Could be worse. Bernie's wife was making him give up red meat all together.

"Fate worse than death," Bernie said. "She's making me eat kale. Kale! Have you ever tried to eat that crap? And brown rice, like white rice ain't good enough no more. Then there's this shit that looks like meat but ain't. Don't know what the world's coming to when a man can't eat meat in his own house."

Bernie snuck away to Rosita's for a stealth burger every now and then. He was supposed to meet up with Marty today, in fact, but so far Bernie hadn't shown. His wife had probably cooked him a nice kale casserole with a side of brown rice and an apple for dessert and wouldn't let him out of the house.

The two punks weren't here for the food. In their dark hoodies, dark jeans, and scuffed up motorcycle boots, they looked like the stoners Marty ran into from time to time at the gas station down the street. Stoners who bought up cheap burritos, taquitos, and candy bars like they were going out of style.

Most people who stopped at the station to get gas gave the stoners a wide berth. Marty didn't. Stoners he could handle. Even old and retired, he could still handle stoners.

The punks weren't stoners though. They were more dangerous than that.

They were here for the money.

Not to rob the place, at least not in the conventional sense. It was a sure bet they were packing, but they weren't wearing masks. Only crazy-ass punks robbed a restaurant full of people in broad daylight.

Even if they just planned to shoot up the place for shits and giggles, they'd still be wearing masks. These days, cameras were everywhere and nobody took any chances.

These two wore the hoods on their hoodies up over plain, dark baseball caps. The hoodies and baseball caps would do a good job of hiding their faces from any overhead security cameras.

All the young punks wore hoodies like it was a damn uniform. In a way it made sense. Loose hoodies hid a multitude of sins, just like the black leather jacket Marty used to wear in his own days doing collection work for old man Guidici.

Marty liked to think he'd been a sharp dresser back then. That leather jacket had been his own uniform, along with black slacks and black shoes he kept shined like they were brand new. He was representing the boss. He had to look good.

Among his other ventures, old man Guidici

had provided protection to the local merchants—dry cleaners, jewelry stores, and restaurants that served as fronts for the real businesses that went on upstairs. Marty and Bernie collected the money Guidici charged those merchants for his services.

The courts would have called what Guidici was doing extortion if anybody had ever got arrested. Guidici paid the cops a fee to look the other way. So Marty and Bernie never even got so much as a hassle from the boys in blue.

The old man knew how to keep everyone happy. No one ever bitched when Marty and Bernie came around to collect the old man's fee. The arrangements were mutually beneficial. The merchants paid Guidici to look out for them. They didn't get robbed. Didn't get hit up by the unions for a kickback on the goods the union guys delivered. The restaurants didn't have to pony up free food to the cops, and businesses with extra-curricular activities didn't get busted.

That had been in the old days.

Marty and Bernie, they'd been retired for a while. The old man had given them a nice pension, told them he wished them well, and said he better not ever hear they'd gone into business for themselves without cutting him in for a percentage.

That was fine with Marty. He was getting too

old for that shit anyway. His knees ached all the damn time. His back felt like a damn tire iron had been shoved in his spine every morning when he first tried to get out of bed. He could never seem to get warm from the minute the leaves fell off the trees in the fall until the first new leaves showed up come spring. He walked a couple of miles a day in a mostly failing effort to keep the weight off. He ate a burger once a week, fish tacos three times a week, and switched to decaf, all to keep his ticker happy.

He'd be damned if he'd eat kale though. A man, even an old man, had to draw the line somewhere.

Guidici had retired himself a couple of years ago and moved down to Florida. He'd left the business to his son. That's how it was done, but in Guidici's case, it had been a mistake.

The kid was a fuck-up who didn't know he was a fuck-up. He paid attention to the wrong things with the business and let other things slide. The old man's lieutenants were still loyal to the family name, but from what Marty heard, some of the rank and file had moved on just like he and Bernie had.

That left the family weak. Easy pickings. Let punks like the two in Rosita's horn in on Guidici territory.

The old man had died in his sleep. Marty hoped

to go that way himself. He'd kept his nose clean since he'd retired. As far as he was concerned, he'd earned a quiet death.

Had the old man known how his kid was running the business into the ground?

If he had, had he cared? Or was that what had killed him?

Marty watched the punks while he pretended to be wholly engaged in eating his tacos. He wasn't packing himself today. The smart thing was simply to watch.

The smarter thing would be to stay out of it.

The punks were somewhere in their twenties. Both white. Not Hispanic. Not Black. Not even Asian. Word was that old man Guidici's kid only had white people working for him. He didn't even hire Italians.

Were these two working for the kid?

The punks walked up to the counter where Rosita rang up her customers after they finished their meals. One of the punks, the one with a face looked like half-cooked oatmeal, said something to her. Marty was sitting too far away to make out the words, but Rosita's expression blanked out. Like someone had flipped a switch and the smiling, charming, happy Rosita disappeared and a stranger had taken her place.

A woman who knew the world would mistreat her if she even thought of letting any emotion show.

Which meant that these punks had done something to her or someone she cared about just to drive home a message. Cooperate or you'll get worse.

Marty'd used intimidation a few times when new merchants moved in and weren't sure they needed the old man's security services. He'd never had to break anyone's legs, him or Bernie. Guidici had been a fair man with those under his protection. He'd also been ruthless with those who crossed him.

Nobody crossed him and lived long enough to talk about it.

These two punks?

They might be here on behalf of old man Guidici's kid. Or maybe they were here on their own. Not that it mattered. Marty knew what was coming next.

Rosita opened the register and took out an envelope. She handed it over to the punk who'd been talking to her, the one with the pockmarked complexion, and he shoved the envelope in his hoodie's front pouch.

Marty didn't have to look inside the envelope to

know it held cash. If Rosita had paid the punks in twenties, he could even make an educated guess as to how much money was inside. He'd worked collections for a long time. The envelope had just enough of a pooch to it that made him think Rosita had just handed over five hundred bucks.

Five hundred was a lot of cash for a diner that only had four booths, six tables, and did most of its business with take-out orders. Old man Guidici's protection fees had always been reasonable and the merchants always got what they paid for. Protection.

Marty didn't think these punks or whoever they worked for—if they worked for anyone besides themselves—could protect Rosita's diner from anything.

He speared a piece of fish out of one of his tacos and ate it slowly. He'd tried to eat a taco once the way you were supposed to. He'd picked it up, got it halfway to his mouth, and most of the insides had fallen out. He'd taken to eating the tacos piece by piece with a fork like a damn barbarian, but at least he didn't end up wearing half his food on his shirt.

The two punks turned away from the counter. The one with the cash ignored everyone inside the diner. Kept his head down and his eyes averted as he headed out the door.

The other one, he was different. He looked around the diner to see if anyone had been watching.

Marty had, and the two of them locked gazes.

The second punk had the eyes of a killer. Flat and dark and totally expressionless.

Back when he'd been on the old man's payroll, Marty had known guys with eyes like that. He'd even been friends with some of them. Get them away from work, get a couple of beers in them, and they seemed just like any other guy you might see in a bar having a good time with his buddies.

But once they were on the job?

Yeah, they had eyes like this second punk.

He'd kill you in a heartbeat and not lose a second of sleep over it.

Sociopaths made great leg breakers. Made for great muscle. They'd do whatever the boss told them to without question.

The first punk, he was the collector. This second guy, he was the muscle. His job was to protect the guy carrying the money.

This second guy was the dangerous one.

Marty wasn't a sociopath, neither was Bernie, but they'd both been dangerous in their own ways. He was old now, sure. He watched what he ate, gave up the cigarettes, and didn't drink much. He walked because it was good for him, not because he liked it. He didn't want to end up in the ground any sooner than he had to.

That didn't make him any less dangerous.

The second punk gave Marty a slight nod. Acknowledgment of one dangerous man to another dangerous man.

Then the punk cocked one hand like a gun pointed straight at Marty. He shot that finger gun at Marty before he followed his buddy outside.

The message was clear.

Stay out of our business, old man, if you don't want me using a real gun on you.

It was good advice.

Marty stabbed another piece of fish. This time he got a piece of shredded cabbage and some of that special sauce Rosita's husband put on the tacos on his fork along with the fish. Good stuff. For fish, anyway.

He chewed slowly while he thought if he should take the punk's advice.

His initial reaction? Fuck, no. No young punk was going to tell him what to do.

The thing was, he didn't need to get mixed up with whatever these punks had going with Rosita and her husband. Maybe they'd gone after her husband with a baseball bat and told him if he didn't want it to happen again, they expected to be paid on a regular basis. Maybe they were actually protecting the place from the gangs that seemed to have taken over this part of the city like they'd taken over parts of most cities it seemed. Marty had no way of knowing.

But there was the other thing.

Marty liked Rosita. She was nice to him. Marty like her husband. He always said hello to Marty whenever he came out of the kitchen while Marty was around. He and Bernie were practically regulars.

Marty wouldn't be able to enjoy himself here, enjoy his food, if he didn't do something—anything—about these two punks, especially the little asshole who'd shot him with a finger gun like he was nothing.

Marty might be old but he wasn't dead

Not yet.

And he intended to stay that way.

Marty and Bernie had been a team back in the day. They'd both started working for old man Guidici around the same time.

Marty'd been a skinny kid who'd gotten in his

share of fights at school, which he always lost. His dad told him to turn the other cheek.

His uncle took him to a neighborhood gym instead where he could learn how to not get his ass handed to him.

That's where he met Bernie.

Bernie wanted to be a boxer. Hell, he was a boxer, but he'd never compete in a ring. His hands weren't fast enough, the trainer said. And he had one more flaw.

He never backed away.

"You gotta dance, in for a quick hit and back out again," the trainer said.

Marty's dad said the guy was full of shit, but what did Marty's dad know about boxing? He was one of those guys who sat on their ass all day long and complained about what everybody else was doing wrong in his book.

The trainer taught Marty how to defend himself. How and where to land a punch to knock a guy flat on his ass in a street fight.

"You gotta hit first," the trainer said. "Before they expect it. While they're still talking shit, trying to intimidate you. If they count to three, you hit 'em on two. Better yet, one and a half. Like—"

Before the trainer said *this*, he head-butted Marty then followed up with a body blow that took

Marty's breath away. Marty had ended up flat on his butt, trying to suck in wind and mostly failing.

"Element of surprise," the trainer said. "If you knew that punch was coming, you could prepare for it. Remember that."

Marty was still flat on his back when Bernie walked over, put his hands on his hips, and stared down at Marty.

"Don't feel bad," Bernie said. "He did the same damn thing to me. It's his schtick."

He reached down with one hand and hauled Marty to his feet.

Even back then Bernie had the kind of muscles a skinny kid like Marty could only dream of having one day. If Marty was a twig, Bernie was a damn old-growth redwood. He wasn't much taller than Marty, but he had the shoulders of a bodybuilder and hands the size of dinner plates. To say he had an air of danger about him was an understatement.

Until he smiled. Bernie had a goofy-ass grin totally at odds with his tough guy appearance. The smile even brought out dimples in his cheeks.

They were roughly the same age. Once the trainer saw how well they got along, he had them work out together. Which mostly amounted to Marty holding the heavy bag while Bernie tried to knock it into the next county. The only thing

Marty was better at was the speed bag. His hands were faster than Bernie's, but he could never get the kind of power into his punches that Bernie could.

Bernie, he punched like a pile driver.

After they'd been going to the gym nearly a year, another one of the gym rats approached them in the locker room.

"I got an opportunity for you boys," he said. "Make some money."

Marty knew how the world worked. He'd seen a lot growing up. Both his father and his uncle worked down at the docks, and they talked a lot when they thought Marty wasn't listening.

"Legal?" he asked the gym rat.

The guy'd given both of them a look. "Does it matter?"

"Gonna get us killed?" Bernie asked. "Arrested?"

"Nope and nope."

"Working for you?" Marty asked.

"Me?" The gym rat smiled. "Naw. Call me a recruiter. There's only one person worth working for when you've got the skills you two boys have."

Marty and Bernie had shared a look. They both knew who he was talking about. You couldn't spend hours at the gym, week in and week out, hanging around a bunch of boxers and wannabes and not know who the guy was talking about.

Old man Guidici.

"So you interested?" the gym rat asked.

Marty hadn't been sure. He didn't have much of a future to look forward to. College was out of the question. His father said he could get Marty a job down at the docks now that he'd put on some muscle and was fast with his hands.

Marty wasn't sure he liked that version of his future, but replacing it with a future working for Guidici? Was that the best he could do?

Bernie had convinced him in the end. Bernie's dad had skipped out on the family when Bernie was little. His mom did okay, but he'd really been counting on making money boxing to help her out. Guidici, Bernie said, treated his people right.

So they went to work running errands. Doing low-level collections. Reporting back any trouble the people under Guidici's protection had with anyone. When there was trouble, Guidici sent someone else to take care of it.

They were a team, and as they got older, Guidici gave them more responsibility.

"Small shit, you take care of it yourself," one of the old man's lieutenants told them. "How you do it is your business, just so long as it don't come back on the old man and becomes his business."

That was their graduation talk. They'd been given the green light to take care of the small shit. Big stuff? Guidici's enforcers would still be taking care of that, which was fine with Marty.

Not that there was a lot of big stuff to take care of. Every now and then someone tried to take over one of Guidici's more lucrative accounts.

They didn't succeed.

Most often there wasn't enough of them left to leave town on their own steam.

The two of them got older, and the older they got, the more responsibility they got. They kept their noses clean. Never did drugs, although drugs seemed to be everywhere, even back then. Beer was better. A few beers a night didn't leave you so fucked in the head that you thought you could skim off the boss.

They met women. Lots of women. Never got serious about any of them until Bernie met the woman who became his wife. He was head over heels after spending ten minutes with her at a bar one night. He'd loved her ever since. He might bitch about her now, especially about her cooking, but he still brought her flowers once a week.

Marty?

He had a cat once. That was it. He'd loved that cat like crazy. Kept it with him for eighteen years until it died of old age in its sleep.

"You need someone to keep you company," Bernie told him more than once. "You're turning into a cranky old bachelor."

Yeah, but he didn't have anybody making him eat kale and fake meat.

Didn't have anybody telling him he couldn't sit around his apartment in his boxers or to turn off the damn oldies station he listened to at night to fall asleep.

Didn't have anybody to make him breakfast in the morning either, but it was a small price to pay for being his own man.

After he paid his lunch tab for his tacos, Marty made a call to Bernie on the way to where he'd parked his car.

"Don't give me shit for not showing up," Bernie said when he answered the call. "She ambushed me."

"Kale?" Marty asked.

"Worse. Cauliflower rice." Bernie made a rude noise that might have been accompanied by an even ruder gesture if they'd been talking in person rather than over the phone. "I was looking forward to that burger," he said in a softer voice. "Don't suppose you had one in my honor."

Marty told him no. He didn't have to say he had tacos. He only ever ate two things at Rosita's. Burgers or fish tacos.

"I called you about something else," he said.

"What kind of something else?"

"Old school stuff," Marty said. "You up for it?"

Bernie snorted. "Sounds like you want to get the band back together."

The marching band. That's what they'd called the old man's crew back in the day. When the band gave you marching orders, you damn well better march.

Would they need the whole band now?

It all depended on whether the punks were working for someone other than themselves.

"Something like that," Marty said. "We just need a little rehearsal time first."

He was stretching the metaphor a little thin, but he figured Bernie would get the message.

"Tell me where and when," Bernie said. "I might even bring a bit of sheet music along. For old time's sake."

They met at a park two blocks south of Rosita's diner. The park had trees and cast iron benches and lawns that had turned winter brown. A few cobblestone walkways meandered through the grassy areas and around trees that had long since lost their leaves to winter.

Marty was hunched up in an old-man overcoat and a woolen cap. He'd even brought along a bag of bird seed. People ignored old folk who came to the park to feed the pigeons. He and Bernie could sit on the bench and talk for hours and no one would think twice about it. The park was a place where they could be anonymous.

Marty had another reason to meet in the park. The bench where they sat gave them a perfect view of the shops along the street for a few blocks in either direction, just in case the punks decided to show their faces.

Bernie had brought along a pistol in the pocket of his own overcoat, a little snub nose .38 revolver that fit nice and neat inside his pocket without causing an obvious bulge. He had other guns at home—the tools of his profession, he called them.

Marty had a good selection of weaponry at his disposal too. You couldn't do the kind of work they'd done for as long as they had without amassing a halfway decent arsenal. He just hadn't gone home to pick any of them up.

He didn't want to miss the punks if they showed up again.

They'd been long gone by the time Marty had finished his lunch and paid Rosita. But if they were making the rounds, collecting from other businesses, chances were good those businesses would be in the same general area.

Marty filled Bernie in on the situation while they waited. When he got to the part where the punk had pointed a finger gun at him, Bernie snorted.

"Punk ass kids," Bernie said. "Don't know what they don't know."

A young mother pushing a stroller jogged past them. The stroller was one of those modern numbers with one wheel out front, two in the back, and a wide grab handle up top. Made for speed. Probably for safety too. The baby inside was bundled up so well it looked like a burrito with a pink hat plopped on one end. The mom wore a knit hat, a thermal jacket, and those yoga pants that showed every curve from her ass down to her ankles. She was in pretty good shape for someone who'd just had a baby.

Or maybe she was just the babysitter.

NOT DEAD YET

Hell, for all Marty knew she could be training for a marathon. More power to her.

Once she'd jogged out of earshot, Bernie said, "You think they're working for Guidici's kid?"

Marty had wondered that himself, but the more he'd thought about it, they didn't seem the type.

"Naw," he said, throwing some seed to the pigeons gathered around the bench. "If they're not independents, they're working for someone new."

They'd made him, but not the way he would expect from someone who worked for Guidici's kid. Marty hadn't been retired all that long, and the kid had been around when Marty was working for the old man. The kid would have told anyone working for him that Marty had long since earned everyone's respect.

"If they're independents, we could let the kid take care of them," Bernie said. "Drop a subtle—"

"It's the kid," Marty said. He didn't trust the kid to do anything right, not like Marty had trusted the old man.

"—or not so subtle word in his ear," Bernie finished. "Keep our hands clean."

Yeah, they could do that. No boss worth his salt —even the kid—would let anyone horn in on his territory. By rights, if Rosita was paying protection to Guidici's kid—and she should have been; the diner was in what had been the old man's territory—word should have gotten back to the kid about what the two punks were doing.

Unless the punks had threatened Rosita and her husband to keep them quiet. That was always a possibility.

But if Guidici's kid got involved, things would get out of hand. Especially if the punks were working for a rival outfit. Wars had started over less.

"First things first," Marty said. "Let's find out who the hell they are."

"You got an idea how to do that?" Bernie asked.

They'd been sitting on the bench for over an hour with no sign of the punks. It was beginning to look like the punks had left the neighborhood. They could sit here the rest of the day and all they'd end up with would be a big lot of nothing.

That left one other option.

Hit up some of their old connections.

The problem was they'd been retired for a while. Old networks dried up when you didn't use them. Didn't grease the right palms on a regular basis.

But some connections never quite went away.

"Yeah," Marty said. "And so do you."

He gave Bernie a look but didn't elaborate.

Bernie would catch on. He always did. Marty just had to give him a minute.

The lightbulb went off in Bernie's brain nearly a minute later. Realization was followed by a sly smile, dimples and all, and then Bernie huffed out a breath that wasn't quite a snort.

"I do," he said.

He stood up and settled his shoulders, like he was getting himself ready to take on a heavy load. Some things, Marty thought, never changed.

Marty's back protested when he hoisted himself to his feet. He'd been sitting too long on the damn iron bench and his back had stiffened up.

"So let's go see the broad," Bernie said.

Marty tossed the rest of the birdseed to the pigeons.

"Think she'll remember me?" Bernie asked.

Marty grinned. "How could she ever forget?"

Cops had informants. Snitches who ratted on fellow degenerates in exchange for a plea deal or at the very least enough cash to score their next hit of whatever mind-altering substances they preferred.

Guys like Marty and Bernie had their own network of spies. Not that they called them that.

They were simply good, upstanding citizens doing their civic duty to keep the neighborhood safe for their fellow man. That's what old man Guidici called them. If they noticed any trouble, they passed the information along to someone who'd get it back to the old man, and then he'd decide what to do about it.

Information was usually exchanged over drinks at a neighborhood bar or a decent meal at a place like Rosita's. Or the gym where Marty had first met Bernie when Bernie was trying to knock the stuffing out of the heavy bag.

This particular upstanding citizen ran a brothel.

Gloria Nicoletti, aka Glory Hallelujah in her working girl days, was pushing sixty herself, but she was still as big and bawdy and buxom as she'd been back when Marty and Bernie were collecting for the old man. She used to trick on the streets until one of the old man's lieutenants took a shine to her. With the old man's blessing, he'd set her up in business on the third floor of a building that housed a dry cleaners and hair salon on the first floor, and a dentist's office and a small accounting firm on the second.

Gloria ran a group of a dozen or so independent contractors, she called them, to whom she rented rooms for the purpose of entertaining their clients. Gloria didn't pimp them out herself. Instead she handled her contractors like a legitimate business. Clients booked appointments through Gloria and paid a deposit up front either from cash reserves that she held on their behalf or though a prepaid credit card like the kind anybody could buy at a corner drugstore.

Her contractors paid a percentage of their take to Gloria for her services. She made sure that percentage was fair, and she also made sure all her contractors were clean. No drugs, no booze, no sexually transmittable diseases. She had a reputation to maintain, and in that she was ruthless.

She was also smart. Early on she agreed to have old man Guidici provide protection for herself and her contractors. He made sure no actual pimp tried to take over her business. He also made sure her business was kept off the cops' official radar.

Gloria's business thrived. None of her girls ever got busted. None of the clients ever got hassled. And nobody but nobody ever said a peep about who those clients were.

Although one time when Marty and Bernie went to collect, Marty could have sworn he passed a high-ranking police official getting on the elevator the same time Marty and Bernie were getting off.

The cop had stared resolutely straight ahead, the adult version of *if I don't look at you, you can't see me*.

Marty had waited until the elevator doors closed before he snickered at the cop's charade. No wonder Gloria's place never got raided. It wasn't just because Guidici had an in with the cops. She had one too.

He used to wonder if the old man had been one of Gloria's own personal clients. Scuttlebutt had it that Gloria had been something else back in her Glory Hallelujah days. As far as anyone knew, she stopped having clients of her own years ago.

That didn't keep her from hitting on Bernie.

Before *and* after he was married.

Bernie never took her up on it. He wasn't a saint, not before he was married, but for whatever reason, he always said no to Gloria. The more he said no, the harder she kept after him. It got to the point that Bernie would stand in the elevator lobby downstairs and wait while Marty went up to the third floor to collect the old man's fee.

One of those times Gloria had let him in on a little not-so-secret secret.

"I'm just doing it to mess with his head," she said.

"You're doing a good job," Marty said. "He don't back down from anybody. Except you."

She handed him the envelope he was there to collect. She didn't always put the money in an envelope. When Bernie was still coming up with Marty to see her, she'd pull the money out from the cleavage between her ample breasts, licking her lips and arching one eyebrow provocatively while she looked Bernie in the eye.

She was the only woman Marty had ever seen who could make Bernie blush.

Bernie, the man who could knock the stuffing out of a heavy bag or crack the ribs of anybody who tried to mess with him without breaking a sweat. Gloria made him blush.

"You gonna wait downstairs?" Marty asked now when the elevator doors opened.

"Hell, no," Bernie said, following Marty into the elevator. "I'm an old fart. What's she gonna want with me?"

Apparently still a lot.

Gloria's face lit up with an honest smile when she saw who got off the elevator.

"My boys!" she said, opening her arms wide. "Come give old Glory a hug."

The front office of Gloria's brothel looked like the front office of any business. Reception desk, a couple of well-padded armchairs. Hell, the place even had a small occasional table between the two chairs complete with recent issue magazines, and not of the titty variety.

Gloria got up from the reception desk and came around to give Marty a hug. Her perfume enveloped him like a softly scented cloud of springtime flowers. Her breasts, still ample things of beauty, pressed against him as she wrapped her arounds around his shoulders.

"Still got the muscles, I see," she said, backing away.

"You're too kind," Marty said. He didn't go to the gym anymore, but he had free weights in his apartment and managed to get in some reps a few times a week. Just in case.

"And what about you?" she asked Bernie. "Do we hug now? Is that a thing?"

Bernie shrugged. He had more color in his cheeks than even when they'd been sitting out on the park bench in the cold.

Marty felt like shaking his head, but he controlled himself. Glory Hallelujah could still make Bernie blush.

"What the hell," Bernie said.

She hugged Bernie far longer than she had with Marty, her hands rubbing his back before they slid up to the short hair at the nape of his neck. From where he was standing, Marty saw her close her eyes and take a nice, deep breath.

When she finally let Bernie go, her smile reached all the way to her eyes, which were just a little shinier than before.

Had she been harboring feelings for Bernie all these years? Wouldn't that be a pisser. Gloria was no hooker with a heart of gold. She was a businesswoman and smart as a whip, but she apparently had a soft spot for Marty's partner.

"You boys aren't on my schedule," she said, "so I'm guessing you're not here for the companionship."

Bernie cleared his throat, but he didn't say anything, so Marty figured it was up to him.

"You always were a smart lady," Marty said.

She laughed, a bawdy chuckle filled with good humor. "Lady now, is it? What happened to 'old broad'?"

"You're too classy for that," he said.

She laughed louder. "I doubt that, but I appreciate the sentiment. So spill it. Why're you here after all this time? I thought you two retired with the big guy's blessing."

"We did," Marty said. "But we've recently become aware of something that might impact the way things are done around here."

Her laughter died. Just like that, she was back in business mode. "Around here, as in here specifically, or here in the neighborhood?"

"Neighborhood," Bernie said. "At least we think it's just the neighborhood."

She glanced back and forth between the two of them. "Tell me what you know," she said. "Then I'll reciprocate, if I've got anything I can share."

So they did.

Marty was getting too old for stakeouts. That's why cops retired and took their pension before they hit sixty. Old bones didn't appreciate sitting in a cold car at eleven at night, waiting for two punk kids to hit the streets.

"Still think we should have told Guidici's kid about this," Bernie said from the passenger seat of Marty's car.

Marty grunted.

"Or at the very least brought some backup," Bernie said. "I don't know about you, but I'm not as sharp as I used to be."

"You're sharp enough," Marty said.

They were both packing, Bernie with the snub nose revolver along with his second favorite gun, a Glock 9mm. He'd also brought along his version of a sap. Marty had his own favorite, a Glock 17. He didn't have a backup piece. If the one gun couldn't do the trick, he figured he'd be dead so what would it matter.

Gloria had given them a lot of information about the two punk kids Marty had seen at Rosita's.

"They're independents," she said. "They've been working the streets around here for the last couple of weeks. They're smart enough not to mess with me, so I've kept my nose out of it. I'm sorry to hear about Rosita. She's good people. All I can say is if the kid knows about them, he's ignoring them for now."

For now.

That could cover a lot of territory. The kid wasn't smart, but he wasn't a hothead either. He liked his business nice and easy. He'd let the situation go on until the punks got cocky enough the kid would have to do something or risk losing his entire business.

Gloria thought the punks were after money to stake themselves in the drug trade. "They're ambitious little shits," she said. "I'll give them that."

Old man Guidici had never dipped his toes in the drug trade. His number one racket was protection. Numbers had dried up once legitimate casinos started popping up everywhere, but he still made decent money operating companies that handled everything from laundry services to garbage collection. And, of course, Gloria's brothel. The kid had inherited those operations. If the kid was ignoring the two punks, it was because they weren't impinging on his various business enterprises enough to make a difference.

Marty thought that was a mistake. If the punks got away with running drugs in the kid's territory, they might start to think the kid was weak enough that they could eventually take over.

That's how cancer started, a little bit at a time. If you didn't hit that shit hard and fast at the beginning, before you knew it, it would be too late to do anything about it short of an all-out war.

Right now it was just the two punks. Who knew how many people they'd have working for them next month. In six months. In a year.

If their drug operation got big enough, they might even entice some of the kid's guys to jump ship. Loyalty wasn't what it used to be when the old man was still running things.

After they'd left Gloria's, Bernie had wanted to

go have a chat with the kid. Marty had nixed that idea.

If they went to the kid with this and he decided to just let it slide, that would be the end of it. Bernie and Marty were old school. The kid had inherited the old man's business. If the kid told them to forget it, they'd have to forget it.

If that happened, the punks would keep hitting Rosita for more and more money in that envelope.

Marty wasn't about to let that happen.

Better to ask forgiveness than permission, if it came to that.

Marty didn't think it would. The kid wasn't totally stupid. As long as what they did couldn't be traced back to him, he'd be fine with it.

Gloria had told them that the punks peddled their shit around a couple of different watering holes frequented by the kind of rough trade who worked in the warehouse district then drank their frustrations away until late into the night.

The night before he and Bernie had staked out a bar that closed at two in the morning, but the punks hadn't shown. Tonight they'd decided to hit the other bar. This one closed at one in the morning.

It was eleven now on a Thursday night, and the bar was still doing a brisk business. The parking lot off to one side of the bar was half full of cars whose drivers would no doubt be too drunk to get behind the wheel.

Not that there were any cops around to stop them.

"We could be inside having a drink," Bernie said.

Marty grunted. "You have a drink now, you'll be out like a light before midnight."

"Fuck you," Bernie said. "You'd deprive a man of one of the few joys left in his life?"

"Let me guess," Marty said. "Kale again?"

He'd picked Bernie up after dinner. Bernie'd had a sour look on his face, which had to mean dinner had been less than spectacular.

"Veggie burgers," Bernie said. "On gluten-free buns. You know what gluten-free buns taste like? Cardboard, that's what."

"Since when have you ever eaten cardboard?"

Marty'd cooked himself a microwave lasagna for dinner. It hadn't been half bad as far as microwave meals went. He'd tried a few over the years that probably could have qualified as cardboard.

"Tonight," Bernie said. "Tonight I ate cardboard."

Bernie was about to get really wound up on his wife-imposed change of diet when Marty spotted two figures in hoodies approaching a group of three men standing on the sidewalk in front of the bar.

"Hey," Marty said. "I think we found our guys."

They'd parked on the street across from the bar and three spaces down. The surrounding neighborhood consisted mostly of warehouses and the kind of small shops that rented space in the warehouse district. A print shop. An appliance repair store. A car rental agency. The businesses were all dark now except for the bar. A perfect spot for drug deals to go down after dark.

They were in the perfect spot to watch it happen.

Marty had a spotting scope he'd bought cheap off a guy a while ago. He'd brought it along tonight just in case. Now it gave him a clear view of the front of the bar.

The cops had to know about this place. It practically screamed dirty deeds, but there wasn't a cop in sight. Maybe it was too small potatoes for the cops. Or maybe the punks had paid them off to look the other way.

Good news for Marty. No cops meant no one in authority was going to interrupt what was about to happen.

"You ready to rock 'n roll?" he asked Bernie.

He got a grunt in response.

Bernie was ready.

Marty was too.

All they needed was for the civilians to get out of the way, then it would be time for two old farts to get to work.

Young punks didn't respect old people. Marty hadn't when he'd been in his twenties.

Old people yammered on about the good old days. About when they were young and strong and powerful.

About when they still mattered.

Nobody younger than forty wanted to hear that shit.

The problem was that old folks didn't respect the young either. Figured they were inexperienced. They'd make mistakes because they let their egos get in the way. Figured they'd be easy marks.

Marty wasn't about to make that mistake with these two.

Especially not with the punk who'd pulled the finger gun on him. That kid had an ego, sure, but he also had the cold, hard, soulless look of a predator who'd killed before and wouldn't hesitate to kill again.

The two were still wearing hoodies, but they'd ditched the baseball caps. The kid with the bad complexion was doing the dealing. Talking up the three men outside the bar. Bouncing a little on the balls of his feet like maybe he'd sampled some of his own product.

The other punk, the one who'd pulled the finger gun on Marty, he was the lookout. He kept watch on the street, the front of the bar, the parking lot. He'd be the one ready for it when it happened.

If it came down to shooting either one of them, he'd be the one Bernie would have to shoot. Marty hoped it wouldn't come down to that. Bernie was retired just like he was. Shooting someone wasn't like choking down some kale or a veggie burger. Shooting someone stayed with you.

Especially since old man Guidici hadn't believed in killing someone from far away.

"You gonna take a man's life," he used to say, "you gotta have the balls to do it close enough he can look you in the eye and see it coming."

Or close enough that when the guy you were supposed to kill turned around to pull a gun on you, you made sure your shot took him down before he could shoot back.

Bernie was good with guns, but he'd only had to shoot someone a few times for the old man. Most of what Bernie did was work people over like he used to work the heavy bag. He only resorted to a gun when a beating didn't take.

Or when someone tried to kill him.

"Hand me the scope," Bernie said.

He looked through the lens while Marty watched the deal go down. One of the men gave some cash to the punk with the bad complexion, and he handed over a small baggie. Without the scope, Marty couldn't tell if the baggie held pills or powder. Not that it mattered. Dope was dope.

"It's the other one, right?" Bernie said. "The guy just watching."

"That's him."

"Bastard's a damn eagle eye," Bernie said. "Ain't gonna be easy to get the drop on them. In this crowd, we'd stand out like a sore thumb."

The civilians weren't going to get out of the way, that much was clear. They looked like working class men who were still wearing the clothes they worked in. Hard drinkers who'd close up the place, go home and grab a few hours' sleep, them report back to work in the morning nursing their hangovers.

The two of them wouldn't be able to just walk up to the bar like they were going in for a drink. They didn't fit in. They should have dressed in dirty jeans and grease-stained jackets. Not that Marty had those kind of clothes.

Plus he figured the watchdog punk would recognize him. If their roles were reversed, he would remember someone like Marty.

"You see where they came from?" Bernie asked.

"Down the street."

The punks had approached the bar from the side away from the parking lot. The area was too isolated, without even a bus route nearby. The punks would have had to drive here just like Marty and Bernie had driven here. They just hadn't left their car in the bar's parking lot.

So where had they left their car?

There weren't any alleyways close to the bar. The warehouses out here were behemoths that stretched nearly a city block long and half as wide, separated by wide asphalt lots big enough to accommodate the semis that had to back into the loading docks.

The other businesses in this area had small parking lots in front, just big enough to hold three or four angled spaces. The punks could have parked in front of any of those businesses. This time of night with all those businesses closed, the punks would have had their choice of prime parking spots.

They could have also parked on the far side of any unhitched trailers left in front of the loading docks, but Marty didn't think so. That would be too far away. The punks would want to park close in case they needed to bug out in a hurry. But not too close.

Marty held out his hand. "Gimme the scope back. I want to check out something."

One thing about this part of town—acreage didn't seem to be at a premium. The street was wide with two travel lanes on both sides and a turn lane in the middle. Blocks stretched on forever, at least four city blocks easy. The buildings didn't crowd up against each other, and streetlights were placed wide apart.

The punks wouldn't risk having to cross five lanes to get to their car, not even with light late-night traffic. So Marty used the scope to check out the darkened businesses on the same side of the street as the bar.

That's when he saw it.

Close to the far end of the block, one of the

streetlights had burned out. There was a car parked under that burned out streetlight.

Marty's eyesight was good for a guy his age. Not great, but good enough he only needed glasses to read fine print. Still, the dark bulk of the car would have been impossible to see with the naked eye.

With the scope?

The car stood out like Bernie's sore thumb.

"Gotcha," Marty said.

"We're in business?" Bernie asked.

Hell, yeah.

"We're in business," Marty said. "Let's go."

Marty parked three spaces away from the punks' car, and they settled in to wait.

The punks would have to walk behind Marty's car to get to their own. Thanks to the burned out streetlight and the fact that the windows in Marty's car were lightly tinted, it would be next to impossible to see Marty sitting in the driver's seat.

Bernie was already out of the car, ready to pull a drunk old man routine. He'd brought a bottle along wrapped in a brown paper bag. The bottle didn't have any booze in it, just water. And enough ball bearings to turn it into a club.

At this time of night there weren't any pedestrians on the street in this neighborhood, but drunks seemed to exist in every part of the city. Chances were the two punks would simply ignore Bernie like people always ignored drunks and bums.

Marty tensed up when he saw the two punks approaching the car. The plan was for him to get out of the car after the two passed behind it. Confront them and ask them nicely to leave good folks like Rosita alone before they bought themselves more trouble than it was worth.

And while their attention was on Marty, Bernie would sneak up on them from behind and put his bottle to good use.

Except, of course, nothing was ever quite that easy.

The two punks walked past the car.

Marty got out.

Only to find the watchdog punk holding a gun on him.

Marty's gun was still in the pocket of his coat. He hadn't wanted to start the conversation off at gunpoint. That had been a mistake.

"Not smart, old man," the punk said.

He was older than Marty originally thought.

His voice was deep, not quite a baritone, but with a rough edge that came from hard living, not genetics. He was holding the gun steady on Marty. Not with that side gangsta grip so many street punks affected, but like a pro with the barrel pointed at Marty's torso.

Bigger target. Better odds.

"You affiliated?" the punk asked.

So they knew about old man Guidici's kid. Knew that they were infringing on the kid's territory. They probably knew that the kid didn't involve himself in the drug trade.

They wanted to know if the kid had decided they were a nuisance after all and sent Marty to dissuade them.

"Retired," Marty said. "You?"

"Not retired," the punk said.

"Affiliated?"

"With ourselves," the other punk said.

He was bouncing on the balls of his feet, his voice a little too loud. A little too in your face.

He was still wired. A dope dealer who used his own product. Not smart, not from a business perspective.

"That true?" Marty asked the punk holding the gun.

"True enough," he said.

There was only a car length between them. Too far for Marty to rush the kid and grapple for the gun. Too close for the kid to miss if he fired.

"I spotted you in your car," the punk said. "Back at the bar. Watching us. If you're so retired, why are you following us? Trying to horn in on our business? Or maybe you got a little side hustle going with that Mexican chick. Afraid we're gonna cramp your style?"

I spotted you.

Not the two of you.

He must not have seen Bernie in the passenger seat back at the bar. He didn't know Marty wasn't out here alone.

Marty didn't look to see where Bernie was. He didn't want the punk with the gun to follow his gaze and figure out Marty wasn't the only one he had to look out for.

"No side hustle," he said. "Rosita's nice folks, and you seem a little greedy."

The punk narrowed his eyes. "And how would you know that?"

Marty shrugged, trying for nonchalance.

It wasn't easy.

It had been a long time since someone had held a gun on him. Especially a stone cold killer. As it turned out, doing this kind of work wasn't just like riding a bicycle. Once you quit riding, getting back on this particular bike didn't come second nature. His shoulders were tense, his neck ached, and a knot had formed in his belly.

Right about the spot where the bullet would hit if the punk pulled the trigger.

"Long experience," Marty said.

"You must have worked for the old man," the punk said.

So he knew old man Guidici too. The punk really was older than Marty had originally thought.

How many people had he killed? Probably not a good thing to think about.

"Must have," Marty agreed.

The other punk's attention was on the conversation now too. Was he an equal partner, or was the punk with the gun the one in charge?

If Marty had been a betting man, he would have pegged the druggie as just a minion. Someone the punk with the gun would dispose of if he became a liability.

Marty caught a brief glimpse of movement out of the corner of his eye. Bernie, getting closer. Getting ready.

Marty made a conscious effort to keep his gaze firmly fixed on the punk holding a gun on him.

"His kid's a joke," the punk with the gun said.

"Weak. That's the word on the street, so we decided to take advantage."

We? Not hardly.

"You two," Marty said, this time letting his gaze shift to the other punk then back again. "You have big plans."

It was absurd, of course. Guidici's kid might not be the sharpest tack in the box, but he wasn't stupid either. If he got pushed into a corner, he'd defend himself. And he had the manpower to do it, but there was no guarantee innocent people like Rosita wouldn't get hurt in the process.

"Dream big," the punk with the gun said. "Make the dream happen."

A brief smile crossed his face, but it was gone so fast it was almost like it hadn't been there at all.

"You have a choice, old man," the punk said. "I let you walk away and I never see you again."

Marty didn't say anything, but the punk was clearly waiting for Marty to provide the obvious response.

So he did.

"Or?" Marty asked. "You gonna shoot me now?"

"Kill you now," the punk said. "Don't want to. I like this gun, and if I kill you, I have to ditch it. So why don't you get back in your car and drive away like the old asshole you are. And while you're at it, find another place to eat. I don't want to see your face again."

The last bit was said as a taunt. Marty knew it, and the punk knew he knew.

"So that's how it is, huh?" Marty said.

"That's how it is," the other punk said. "Now get the fuck out of here so we can get on with our business."

Bernie claimed he wasn't as sharp as he used to be. But he was sharp enough. And light enough on his feet. He had never danced away in the boxing ring like the trainer had wanted him to, but close in fast? That much Bernie could always do. Even now.

And he still packed a hell of a punch.

The two punks were so focused on Marty, on seeing whether he'd make a move, that they never heard Bernie coming.

Bernie threw a jackhammer of a punch into the druggie's kidneys that dropped him to his knees, howling in pain.

Before the punk with the gun got his head halfway around to see what the hell was going on, Bernie swung the bottle with the ball bearings right at the side of the punk's head.

The solid weight of the loaded bottle crashed into the punk's skull at the temple and caved it in.

The punk's fingers squeezed reflexively on the trigger as he went down.

He was dead before he hit the pavement.

The bullet shattered the driver's side window of Marty's car, but it missed him.

Bernie dropped the bottle, shattered now, water leaking through the paper bag, and pulled his revolver on the second punk. He was still on his knees, tears streaming down his cheeks, snot running from his nose.

"Don't shoot me," the punk said, hands held out in front of his face like they could stop a bullet. "Don't shoot me. I have money. I can pay you."

"Quit your sniveling," Bernie said, "or I might shoot you just to shut you up."

They didn't have a lot of time. The city had one of those high-tech gunshot reporting systems these days. If the cops hadn't been paid off to ignore any gunfire reported in this area, they'd eventually show up to check things out.

Marty pulled out his own gun and held it on the punk.

"Listen up," he said. "You're going to leave town. Take your trade and do it elsewhere. All I want back is what you took from Rosita."

The punk looked at him with scared eyes. "Who?"

"The woman at the Mexican restaurant," Marty said.

The punk shook his head. "We don't got that envelope no more."

Of course not.

"I can give you what we made tonight," the punk said. "You can have it, all of it. I don't know if it's enough. I never saw how much was in the envelope she gave me."

Marty hadn't looked inside the envelopes he'd collected for the old man either.

"Hand it over," he said.

The punk handed a wad of bills to Bernie, who stuffed them in the pocket of his overcoat without taking his gun off the punk.

"Now drive away," Marty said.

The punk glanced down at where his partner—his boss—was bleeding out on the asphalt. "I don't got the keys. He does."

"Then I guess you better run," Bernie said.

When the punk didn't move, Marty said, "Now, asshole."

The punk ran, hunched over to one side, his gait unsteady.

"Think you ruptured his kidney?" Marty asked

as they got back in his car.

"Maybe," Bernie said. "Got my adrenaline up. I probably hit him harder than I needed to."

Marty couldn't make himself feel bad about that, just like he couldn't make himself feel bad about the punk Bernie had killed. A guy like that wouldn't have let him drive away. He'd let Marty get in the car, and then he'd put a bullet into Marty's brain.

Just to send a message to whoever they were working for.

Marty drove back to the city proper. He kept to the speed limit. Made a full stop at all stop signs even if there was no traffic. Looked both ways when traffic lights turned green just to make sure nobody was going to run the red in the opposite direction.

The driver's side window on the car was shattered. The bullet itself was probably embedded somewhere in the car. He'd look for it in the morning and dig it out. Before they'd left the little parking lot behind, he'd knocked out enough safety glass so that what was left wouldn't have an obvious bullet hole. He didn't want anybody asking questions when he took the car in to have the window repaired.

It was almost midnight and thanks to the

busted window, the car was freezing. He'd have to take a hot shower when he got home just to warm up enough to crawl into bed, otherwise his entire body would be a mass of stiff, aching muscles in the morning.

Was he getting too old for this kind of work? Maybe.

But he wasn't dead yet. Neither of them were. And they'd both been good enough to do what needed to be done.

Tomorrow he'd go see the kid and let him know what went down. Just as a courtesy. A matter of respect.

Then he'd go have lunch at Rosita's. A burger this time, he decided. Fuck the fish. He deserved two thick beef patties cooked medium rare. He deserved extra cheese, bacon, and a sour pickle on the side. Maybe he'd asked Rosita for extra bacon too. Her husband would make the burger like that if Marty asked.

Bernie might even be able to get away and join him for lunch.

If his wife let him out of the house.

Marty wanted to celebrate being alive. He wanted to eat food he shouldn't because what the hell, eating food that tasted good even if it wasn't good for you was part of living the good life. They'd say hello to Rosita and her husband, and maybe even order dessert.

And when they left?

They'd make sure to leave her a hell of a good tip.

READ MORE!

Never miss an issue of Mystery, Crime, and Mayhem! Get yourself a subscription!

READ MORE!

https://www.mysterycrimeandmayhem.com/product/mcm-subscription/

For the latest news, sign up for the newsletter here:

https://www.mysterycrimeandmayhem.com/never-miss-a-release/

In addition to learning about all the great issues, you'll also get a free copy of the *MCM Criminally Good Anthology*.

READ MORE!

OUR FRIENDS

Friends of MCM
    Knotted Road Press
    Pub Share
    BookFunnel
    Thrill Ride The Magazine
    Sisters in Crime
    I Found This Great Book
    Crime Writers of Color
    One House Productions

www.ingramcontent.com/pod-product-compliance
Lightning Source LLC
LaVergne TN
LVHW021756060526
838201LV00058B/3112